DREAMS OF MONTEZUMA

DREAMS OF MONTEZUMA
Copyright © 2020

ISBN: 978-1-7340126-1-3
Library of Congress Data Available on Request

First paperback edition published by Stalking Horse Press, in collaboration with New Mexico School for the Arts, May 2020

All rights reserved by respective authors. Except for brief passages quoted for review or academic purposes, no part of this book may be reproduced, stored in a retrieval system, or transmitted by any means without the written permission of the publisher. Published in the United States by Stalking Horse Press.

The characters and events in this book are fictitious or used fictitiously. Any similarity to real persons, living or dead, is coincidental and not intended by the author. The opinions expressed herein are those of the authors, and not intended to represent the opinions of New Mexico School for the Arts. Proceeds from any sales of this book by Stalking Horse Press will be donated to the Creative Writing and Literature department at NMSA.

www.stalkinghorsepress.com
www.nmschoolforthearts.org

Design by James Reich

Stalking Horse Press
Santa Fe, New Mexico

DREAMS OF MONTEZUMA

AN ANTHOLOGY OF POETRY AND PROSE BY CREATIVE WRITING AND LITERATURE STUDENTS AT NEW MEXICO SCHOOL FOR THE ARTS
SPRING 2020

STALKING HORSE PRESS
SANTA FE, NEW MEXICO

CONTENTS

Oz Leshem
Lancaster — 9
A Quarter Tank of Gas, If It Is Even Necessary — 16

Satya Kutsko
Bitter Coffee — 19

Artemisio Romero y Carver
Speech #4 | For use at Funerals and Interventions — 25
Speech #9 | For use on Governors and State Representatives — 27

Sarah Peralta
Blueberry Hill — 29

Lucy Wilson
Sailors' Patches — 35
Remember — 36
Escapee — 37

Skye Bowdon
Arsonist — 39
Deception — 40
Seeds — 41

Dakota Rose
Vanilla Tears — 43

ANNABELLA HILL
NOVACAINE — 47

SARITA GONZALEZ
1939 — 51
ELEVEN — 54
IVORY 505 — 57
SAVE — 59

MYLIE JONES
THE LAST GLASS — 61

ISABELLA FLETCHER
MELANCHOLY — 69
STOLEN — 71

LUCIA ROSEN
WE TOOK FLIGHT — 73

SEAN MONTOYA
BLAME — 77

ADRIENNE RUGG
INCUBUS — 81
FEAR OF FALLING — 83
THE MOTH — 84
IN WAR — 85

GIOVANNA KALANGIS
BLURRED — 87

Pearl Cook
127 — 93

Annabella Hill
The Doll Kingdom — 95

Satya Kutsko
Stuck — 103

Gabriel Boston-Friedman
That Word — 107
Futures — 109
Endless Destinations — 110
What Happens When You Ask Questions — 112

Skye Bowdon
What Your Country Can Do for You — 115

Malia Seva
Untitled — 119

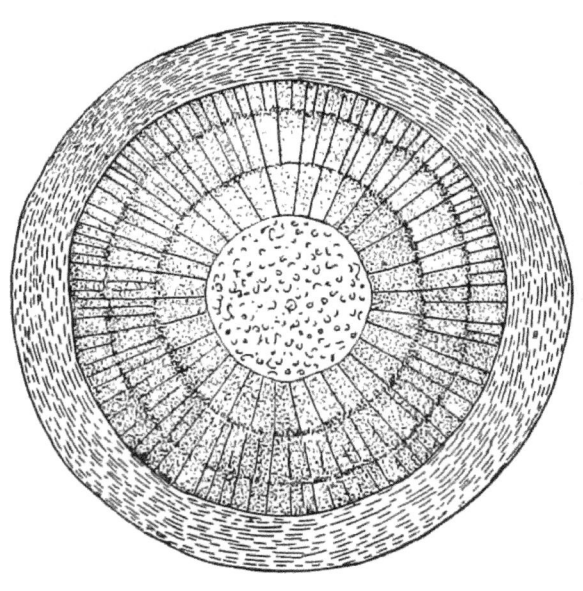

OZ LESHEM

LANCASTER

LANCASTER

\\\//\\\//\\\//\\\//\\\//\\\//\\\//\\\//\\\//\\\

I: *inertia's opposite*

— a mountain is a myth — ideas are myths and myths are always ideas — so mountains might really be myths — ego is for everyone — but do we express it — do we express our inner animal — do we express what is inside the clattered shell of human flesh — what is really our flesh — what is inside earth's core — away among saturn a way among universe a way to be among an axis of opaque hues — conjoin — a midpoint joining two — creating a circuit — axis mundi beyond a geocentric coordinate — *line or stem through the earth's center connecting its surface to the underworld and the heavens and around which the universe revolves* — a mountain — the connection of two worlds' ends —

---

con·nec·tion
/kəˈnekSH(ə)n/
noun
1. *a relationship in which a person, thing, or idea is linked or associated with something else.*
2. *a supplier of narcotics.*

— i always grew up wondering why i had such a connection to the mountains — constantly wondering how i was able to feel so free yet be so enclosed by them — taos — a little town in northern new mexico — it had the narcos native americans stoners hispanics crackheads whites drug dealers teenage alcoholics — hippies — we are called taoseños — the northerners but also southwesterners — i never really understood where i'd fit in but i always found some sort of oddball or outcast to hang around — but the one place i really felt accepted was in the taos mountain range — i often hear cacophonies rise from them — ever changing with the many different forms of humanity — the middle — the brink edge of the gods — farther than opposites we've come to believe — heaven — hell —

— a midpoint —

— and it creates a far revolving circle of some vulgarity —
in its stigmata —

— the one problem i came across the most — the tangled web of my relationship with my father — clashing yet so far — it was as if narcissism sought out a new connotation every day — came shrouded in shame — almost like a rabid animal caged inside me — scraping flesh slowly and slowly until — it finally — reached the brink of the dermis — just cutting the sephardic complexion of my skin — but i feel it wait for each little drop of blood to hit the ground until it coagulates — then breaking out of my rib cage to just fall on the ground shivering — weak and small with a young mind but aged body — *visualized immaturity* — plotting scheming its whole life in the dark but when finally shone light — it freezes — as frozen as the smile on the bleak mother-in-law's face as she greets her son's new husband —

— as this animal wakes — it makes its unconscious way to the edge of the mountain — seeking its own axis mundi — its own midpoint of sanity — just to be thrown out of the brink — into a cage of the underworld — eternity is what i would call it — but again — what would that really be — what would that really do with the polarity of the mountain's midpoint to its summit —

---

rad·i·cal·ism
/ˈradəkəˈlizəm/
noun
1. *the beliefs or actions of people who advocate thorough or complete political or social reform.*

— the day i left — the little sense of freedom i've ever felt — never really understood that kind of rush through my body — thinking about how it would affect your life — how blurred the lines would get without you by my side — salvaging each little memory of you in my childhood — i finally realized — your lies crawled inside the tender heart i thought — you had — but i still left — i'd rather call it fleeing — from all the manipulation and heartache — fleeing from my past self — fleeing from a mental constraint — a thought of being unable to strengthen an azure soul — unable to escape this purgatory of our minds — stuck in the middle — of what we call — paradise —

///\\\//\\\//\\\//\\\//\\\//\\\//\\\//\\\//\\\/

II: *for ink*

— density — creates connections to form in my mind — i never understood what i could do with ink until i realized its meaning in my life — ink to me — is the bridge that connects my mind to the outside world — often we tend to keep our thoughts in our minds — i write them down — ink is a fluent stream passing through cities

— it is a map that gives you directions to the enlightenment of the mountains — it is the radical of every religion — the radicalism of every generation — it is the society in which i am an outcast to — it is why i connect with the mountains — i would define ink as — the vernacular of my mind —

— a strange ample thought controls me — hassan-i-sabbah — assassin in the mountains — *of the nizari ismaili state and its fedayeen military group known as* — *order of assassins* — of it bred philosophy to justify society — incredibly probable — i escape a lunar dilation in the filming of something so pulp — hassan-i-sabbah — to assassinate is to kill — but to execute is to exit — kill to execute — assassinate to execute — execute because kill — because assassination isn't good enough for you — so we exit — gentrify — they can't see the sky swimming — resorting to militants — perhaps — your vowel on lifetime —

— cadence of his tingling notions —

— purely vile imagination — nonexistent fluidity in the socialism of altruistic motion — want their name in the lights — guess i'd want that too — but as a mechanism of plausible connection — a system not broken — but set up to be restricted by the dismissal of all things different —

— there is an intimacy of the connectionbetween ink and mountains —a line drawn at the summits — creating a *range* — as for ink creates its landscape —

ar·dor
/ˈärdər/
noun
1. *enthusiasm or passion.*

— therefore it is so important to consider this question —

— what do you desire —

///\\\//\\\//\\\//\\\//\\\//\\\//\\\//\\\//\\\//

III: *sing about me, i'm dying of thirst*

— for a radical — an immortal man is not something they desire — but something they hope to achieve — a radical's views number a multitude of when how and what something is —

— i'll probably die to defuse —

pre·car·i·ous
/prəˈkerēəs/
adjective
1. *not securely held or in position; dangerously likely to fall or collapse.*

— for the ambiguity of a person is not something to hold onto — but something to juxtapose in the variables it creates — because we never truly understand how separate individuals react — it falls —

cracks from the base — the soliloquy of its instability shows more than the other side — kind of like a mountain's surface — crackled rusty particles descending off as the moon shines in its direction — shining as if it was a piece of glitter stuck between the cracks of a table to divide it in half —

— aristotle never knew the true meaning of poetics — nor did dickinson — but it was the ink that changes their perceptions — how they concluded their ideas — how they examined a mountain —

— how they controlled their prophecies —

— when i left — i went to the town of santa fe — a little town just an hour and a half south of taos — this town truly changed my life — i went to go to high school — new mexico school for the arts — now — i heard about this school my whole life — growing up in taos we never think about these things — making art in any form as a teenager in taos is obscure — odd — gay — but i always loved art — it is what drove me and saved my life — without art — none of this would be here — this school was filled with creative wild goofy abstract individuals — i desired to be in a place where being an outcast was the norm — dance theatre music visual arts creative writing — any passion you had in art — you could probably do it at that school — being in the school changed my perception of life and how humans process community and society's troubles — being a teenager in this environment made me who i am today — people tend to have a hard time processing freedom — although it is accepted all around the world —

— imagine having the chance to fulfill all your dreams without anyone telling you that you shouldn't do that —

— for something so simple — was the hardest thing anyone ever had to do —

anx·i·e·ty

/aNG'zīədē/
noun
1. a feeling of worry, nervousness, or unease, typically about an imminent event or something with an uncertain outcome.

— an aura you create — stuck in an illusion of time — a fear of the world — a fear of what we cannot control — a fear of something strange — perhaps it is something we know nothing about — or maybe it is something that'll be taken away —

— your nailpolish is my tears —

— and for now —

— we always find a way to go back to that mountain — the same one my brother fractured his leg on — the same mountain i was too scared to kiss you on — the same one my whole town skied on — the same one holding a militia of assassins — with hassan — the same one i inked a landscape of — the skyline of mountains that peaked over the clouds — slicing the fog —

— that mountain —

— the same mountain that shifted the everchanging light of our solitude —

A QUARTER TANK OF GAS, IF IT IS EVEN NECESSARY

1.4677: Make sure the water skims your dry, pale arm
                when you   feel sick
1.4678: Not like the inclined motifs
                that passed away from   other generations to mine

1.4679: Our bodies are captured

                      entwined with my heart;

                                tethered to your silhouette

1.4680: I gave you my heart

                    1.4681: Remember that.

1.4682: Please,
        never forget
1.4683: You   tugged   on my chains
                    1.4684: You need to stop

1.4685: You dictate my crest   engraved inside you
1.4686: The crest's slick smooth metal   impaled in your fleshy meat
    with stabs   like the ones   *in my*   *back*

                              1.4687: Try it if it feels right
1.4688: I have seen   your hopes   rot,
      rot   like the breath   of your lilac heart
      D E C A Y E D
1.4689: this half-eaten apple   nobody will ever eat it

        never   going to touch it
        taste it

                          1.4690: Except for you
                                you taste it
and I taste your lips

1.4691: This feeling
        The strongest feeling   something that holds us
        together
1.4692: Infatuated   with the

succulent mystery of this   poetic paradox of your body

1.4693: At sunset   we found an
                            1.4694: Extrapolated euphoria
    a hyperbolic aroma   of your hair

1.4695: I don't sleep
        not because of insomnia
        because I can't imagine a world
                without you
                      your voice
                          your smile
                              your eyes
                                1.4696: You got what I want
                                You are why I am

                So thirsty.

                                  —Oz Leshem

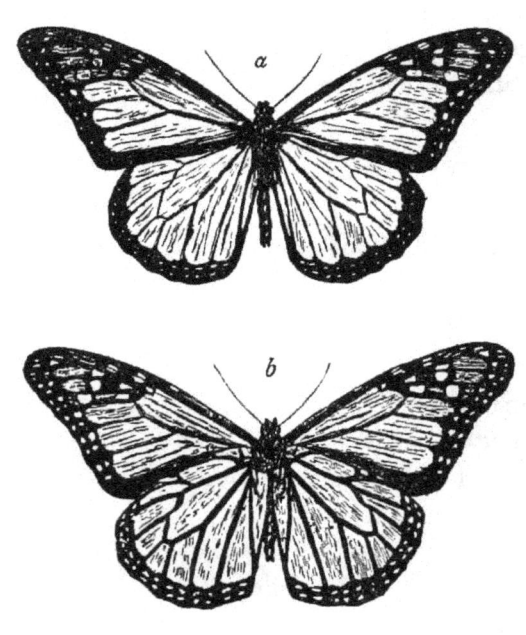

SATYA KUTSKO

BITTER COFFEE

The tour bus soared over the endless yellow plains. The white paint on its left side needed some touching up. As a Led Zeppelin song played on the radio, the bus swerved onto the rumble strips for the third time that hour. The road was ragged and needed paving. Inside, at the back of the bus with its beige carpeted walls, a vent rattled above a glittering red backdrop. On the front of the bus, a sign displayed HEARTACHE TOUR - 1973. The passengers were silent, or dead-asleep. Except for one man, leaning his head against the window. His ginger curls fell past his ears, framing a pair of star-shaped sunglasses on his pink, Romanian nose. He stared over the plains, pine green eyes, looking for something. Anything. His expression was blank. Three rings hugged his freckled fingers on his right hand. A gold chain watch hung on his left. The watch read 2:30 p.m. He tapped his pointer finger impatiently. They passed another green sign.

FLAGSTAFF 70 MILES

JCT. 16 120 MILES

WINSLOW 160 MILES

"Really? Seventy miles until we reach civilization?" he said, in an annoyed, northern accent. *Over there, something approaching in the distance.* "Roy..." He scampered down the narrow aisle to the bus driver. "Roy, see that over there? Stop the bus."

A man in a stark, black pinstripe suit stood up, irritated. "Levon—"

"Stop the bus!"

The bus swerved onto the exit ramp. At the bottom of the incline lay a teal-painted motel, and a rest stop.

"You're on stage in five hours," the suit protested.

"You know what, Robby? I don't care. I just need a cup of coffee, or else I'll go berserk."

"Levon—"

Levon shoved past him, rushing down the bus stairs, and standing, for a moment, with his back to the open doors.

Behind him, still on the bus, Robert and Roy conferred. Robert said he'd take care of this. Roy said he'd fill up the bus. Robert said that was excellent, and descended metal stairs, walking after Levon who had started for the rest stop building. The bell on the door rang as he entered the store.

"Thank god." Levon ran over to the coffee station.

Ding ding.

Robert said, "Alright, Levon. We gotta go."

"Why? You said it yourself: we have 5 hours." Levon poured coffee into a Styrofoam cup.

"Levon. You remember what happened the last time we-"

"The last time we stopped, you told me to go back to sleep, so I did." As he reached for the cream, Robert slapped his hand away. "Hey!"

"Not that time, man. The time before that."

"It was no big deal! That man doesn't represent everyone in suburbia."

"I know he doesn't, but your face—"

"—was just puffy from the *performance*. It's gone now, you see? No big deal."

"Levon…"

"I just want some coffee, Robby, damn it."

They stood in silence.

Robert ushered Levon towards the gray checkout counter. "Ever since that radio show, people…" He stopped in the middle of the floor. "People are looking at…us."

"People *always* look at us."

"That's not what I mean," Robert said, pulling Levon closer, lowering his voice to a whisper. "If people find out about you and me, your career is over."

"You mean that *your* career is over. When have you ever cared about me?"

"That's not the point. It's 1973, Levon."

"Of course it is, Robby. I read it on a calendar."

Robert blushed with rage, gripping Levon's forearm. "You're a child."

Before he could continue, another voice cut in. "Excuse me, sir?"

The men turned to the greasy teenager behind the counter.

"Are you Levon Haynes?" the kid said.

Robert released his arm and Levon moved forward. "Yeah."

"Oh, wow, I'm such a big fan!"

"Hey, thanks."

Robert pulled him back, again. "Yeah, he's performing in a few hours. We have to get back on the bus." Outside, Roy had finished refueling and was kicking dust.

"Well, aren't you going to pay?"

Robert nodded, embarrassed. "Ah... yes, of course."

Levon moved closer to the counter, thumbing bills from his wallet, only to have Robert push him aside.

"Will that be all for you?"

"Actually..." Robert walked over to a rack and grabbed two bags of Corn Nuts, "I'll also have these."

"I—I hate to ask," the kid began. He looked past Robert's shoulder, to Levon. "But, can I have an autograph?"

"Sure." Levon reached over the register for the kid's sharpie. "Let's see. What can I write on?"

The kid handed him a glossy postcard with "ARIZONA, The Grand Canyon State!" in goofy bubble lettering. "Here!"

Robert exhaled, and shuffled, antsier than ever to escape.

"What's your name, kid?"

"Adam."

"A—dam." Levon finished off the signature with a large star.

To Adam,

Always reach for the stars.

—Levon Haynes

Adam thanked them both.

Robert mustered up his last bit of kindness before snatching the corn nut bags, and pushing Levon towards the door. "It's always wonderful to meet a fan."

Adam waved goodbye, smiling and holding the postcard close to his heart.

Ding ding.

Levon giggled when they got out of the store. Sipping his coffee, he pouted, "It's bitter."

Robert slapped the coffee out of his hand and grasped Levon's wrists. "Now, we have to get to Phoenix in under 5 hours, idiot."

"Now, who's fault is that, *Mr. Manager, sir?*"

Levon shrugged him off, and started to walk back to the bus, leaving footprints of coffee on the black pavement.

Robert pulled him back.

"If you do that *one more time*, Robert, I swear—"

Slap.

"Get back on the bus."

"Robby…"

Ignored.

"Robby..."

Ignored, again.

Levon looked back to the coffee drying into the concrete. They boarded the bus and Roy started the engine. Robert ushered Levon to the back and sat him down under the glittering red backdrop.

"I'm sorry." Robert tried to sound sincere. "I understand how hard it is to be...well, you..."

Some hope sparked in Levon's heart.

"But, I'm just too angry to talk to you, right now." He walked down the aisle to his seat, leaving Levon alone, once again.

Levon adjusted his sunglasses and stared through the hot window at the blue sky and endless yellow plains. "It's okay."

Robert turned around to watch a single tear fall from beneath Levon's star-shaped shades.

Levon licked at it when it neared his lips.

"The coffee was bitter, anyways."

—*Satya Kutsko*

ARTEMISIO ROMERO Y CARVER

2 POEMS

SPEECH #4 | *For use at Funerals and Interventions*

Grandma said

        Chico, we weren't always like this

Then Aunt said

    Timmy passed, we don't know if it was the drugs or the alcohol

Blue blooded redneck with purple varicose veins
Never tongue tied black necktied hands stained
hands untrained
in hard work
My art work
done claimed
stuff it can't name

I can't name the monolith lack of consciousness that done claimed you
My blood bubbling and boiling over
Toiling over the same bone dry land
Opportunities to some are buckets in the pouring rain
To you it was speeding up in a single lane

...

blocked up highway
I say all this
as just another hypocrite
Year ago on I saw you

on the street, hand to mouth, feet to asphalt, back to me, clear to see

the ongoing transfusion
I knew you were using
Could have said something, instead
I walked away
I knew that day that you were already dead,

Never could account for all the president's men
All the precedents been
set against
little kids with the last name
Martinez,
        Chavez,
                Romero

So why not shoot heroin
like cupid shoots arrows

SPEECH #9 | *For use on Governors and State Representatives*

Pray for me, pray for me,
You said I should work hard go to college
So who on god's earth is gonna pay for me
maybe scholarship
or white grandparent
or maybe I sell my soul
I know I can't pay it
back`
Pay it back
Story of my life is a rough draft

Pray for him, pray for him
Cesar Chavez never got a day for him
oil painting with the gold leaf frame made for him
or an apology
His biography is just the same story
Say sorry
Why won't you just say sorry?

Pray for you, pray for you
You can call yourself a politician
but we got other names for you
If there weren't children present
I would say a few
I would scream at you
you broke my people in two
You killed Timmy
and you got the nerve to think you've earned
a photo op and a handshake wit me

...

You want to show me a brighter future

but I know it's pay per view
On voting day you say that I should go to your church, take a ballot and pray for you.

—Artemisio Romero y Carver

SARAH PERALTA

BLUEBERRY HILL

It's funny how your perception of time changes as years pass. Or maybe it isn't. It's only logical that, as time passes and you experience more things, your brain might let go of the memories that are no longer relevant in your day-to-day life. The human mind, perceived to be incredible, cannot remember the exact things you did, even if it was only yesterday. And of those memories that you hold on to, why are they always the bad ones? Why do we tend to remember the frightening and unpleasant ones?

*

There's not much I remember about the State Fair. The last time I went I was around seven. I remember the crowds, and how hot it was. I remember going late at night and playing games with my friends. My grandpa did something for it. I don't really remember now. I know he was important because he had a trailer in the Fair that we could go into. That was my mom's favorite part because the state fairs are hot. I doubt I ever really liked the State Fair. Crowds were never my favorite. Neither was the summer.

The first New Mexico State Fair happened in 1938. When it opened, it cost only 35 cents for adults and 15 for children. If my grandparents had gone, they would have been paying about that much.

*

My grandparents grew up in an area we now call Taos, in New

Mexico. At the time, Taos was divided into smaller parts that functioned like their own towns. My grandpa was born in the town of Taos, growing up in the central life source. My grandma was born in Ranchos de Taos, just south of the town. Growing up, she rarely went into the town, only going for fiestas, or other special events.

✴

Fiestas are a piece of New Mexican history that are interwoven into the culture. Thinking about it now, they are quite morbid in their meaning and what they represent. The fiestas are a celebration of the reconquest of New Mexico by the Spanish. There are parades of people dressed in 17th-century clothing, reenacting resettlement. These people are often accompanied by la Reina and her court, including princesses and princes. In order to be la Reina, you must be of the Catholic faith, with a Spanish surname and lineage.

Fiestas are sweaty and crowded. People come from all over to celebrate under the hot sun. The streets around the Plaza are crammed with vendors selling cheap earrings and funnel cakes. The Rotary Club is always there, with a carousel. The carousel used to be my favorite thing. All those horses that wind around the pole, forever a slave to the wheel. In the parade, people ride through on horseback. I had a friend who used to ride through the parades. She's in college now. My grandparents were on floats sometimes, too. Everything is brightly-colored and you can feel the sun beating down on your back. The food there is gigantic. I once got a burrito that was two feet long. Or, at least, that's how I remember it.

✴

I think one of the most incredible things about my grandparents is their selflessness. It doesn't matter what they are going through, they still find ways to help the community. One of the ways my grandma has always contributed is by participating in the Taos branch of the Rotary Club. My grandma has been part of it for 21 years, longer than I've been alive. She was also its first female president, more proof that she is truly incredible. The Taos Milagro Rotary Club does lots of things. They go into the public schools and read to children. They donated dictionaries to every child in my third-grade class. My grandma was the 2012 Unsung Hero of Taos, and when she got the award she was as humble as ever.

"I said 'no, I'm not unsung,'" Peralta recalls saying, during the conversation with *The Taos News* editor Joan Livingston. "Everybody knows me, and everybody knows what we do, and that we've been involved within the community."

They believe that the town has done so much for them, that it is only right for them to give back, in any way they can.

*

Once they were high school age, both of my grandparents went to Taos High School in the heart of Taos. It was in a building that is now used as an elementary school named Enos that my dad went to, and my mom used to work at. They both went there from 10th to 12th grade, the first point in time they were in the same place. My grandma is eight months older than my grandpa so they were never in the same classes. She graduated in 1963, and he in 1964.

In high school, my grandpa had the nickname of Gov. When I first found this out, I laughed at the almost prophetic nickname. My grandpa was never the governor of anything, but he was the Mayor of Taos. Somehow, this childhood nickname had predicted his career in politics.

Even though they were going to the same school, they never actually knew each other personally. My grandma always says that she had heard of him because he was so smart, but didn't really know who he was. They didn't meet until a couple years after they both graduated. And not in New Mexico either. No, my grandparents who grew up in a tiny town, who went to the same high school, only met at a party in Racine, Wisconsin.

*

At the time, Racine had a population of 89,144, a number which is higher than it is today. Racine sits on the edge of Lake Michigan, at the beginning of the Root River. When my grandparents met, my grandma was planning on becoming a nun. My grandpa got a degree in philosophy and had started working towards becoming a college professor.

*

No matter how much I think about it, it still blows my mind that two people from the same town met in another town 1,035 miles away. I guess it was just meant to be.

*

I've always wanted to escape. I've never been one to fully appreciate the life I am living. Every ounce of my being has been formed by the things I have escaped from, and the places where I went. I have always got lost in books and movies, taking refuge in the pages. Characters go on grand adventures through the world, making friends and enemies. My life is not a particularly interesting one. So, I bury myself in the stories and lives of other people.

I think this is why I have always been fascinated by stories. Not fictional ones, but ones where you can feel the memories reaching out and grabbing at you. That's how I feel every time I am around my dad's family. I can just feel the history and stories that live inside their bones. Every time they talk, I make sure to listen. I hope one day I will have those stories weaving in and out of my every step.

*

I got to see my grandma last night. She picked me up and we went out to dinner. The name of the restaurant and what we got is not important, because that is not what this story is about. My grandma has lived through many things, and I always look forward to the story she will inevitably tell when I am with her. I love listening to stories about her childhood or my dad's or aunts' or uncle's. But, last night, she told me a story from when she was younger; younger than me.

*

She was alone. Or at least it felt like she was. Her father was away working, and the only people in the house were her mother and younger siblings. She lay in her parents' bed, next to her mother's sleeping form. She had awoken with a start when a loud banging traveled up the steps. She thought maybe her father was home, but after the noise didn't stop, she grew scared. There was someone in her house. Her mother woke up soon after, and they both sat in the bed, afraid. She cracked open the door and looked down at the steps that led to the lower level of the house. She could see a man flicking on a lighter to light his path up the stairs.

She closed the door as quietly as she could. Her sister lived nearby. She could go there to call the police. She climbed out the window as rain poured from the sky. The wind pushed the cold rain into her as she ran across the fields to her sister's house.

While this was all happening, her two younger siblings had managed to get into the same room as each other, and climbed onto the roof, in hopes of being safe up there. Her mother had climbed on top of a portal protruding from their house. She started inching down the terrace, but she slipped and fell on her back. Her mother got up anyway and ran to her sister's house. Her mother had actually hurt her back pretty seriously and had to go to the hospital the next day.

She banged on her sister's door, close to three a.m. They called the sheriff and he showed up, ready to find the trespasser.

But things are not always as they seem. You see, the intruder was never actually an intruder at all. Or at least, he didn't mean to be. The man turned out to be a neighbor who lived nearby. He was drunk, stumbling home in the dark. He thought he was in his own house.

My grandma still remembers when he came back. She remembers him crying and how much that broke her heart, to see a grown man cry.

*

The stories that we tell are important. They help us define who we are and where we came from. They might not always be clear, they might not always have all the pieces in the right order, but they always come from the heart. We can't let go of our stories because we are nothing without them. We are all creatures formed by stories. Even if you feel like yours hasn't begun yet, you have the ones of those before you. The stories of those before me connect me to my home and help me remember,

> where I came from.

— Sarah Peralta

LUCY WILSON

3 POEMS

SAILORS' PATCHES

Walking the pier
Fingers woven
Careful stitching

Shoulders brush
Static electricity
Illuminating sail cloth

Threads of lightning
Striking the sand
Glass statues

Salt envelops old wood
Splinters bury into soles
Pin pricks to toes

Tears fall
Cracking black water
Waves break on drunken legs

Stars tilt
Dark seas open
Seams rip on the seabed.

REMEMBER

lost,
stumbling around my mind.
i remember holding your hand,
walking towards the flashing lights.
we walked down the chipped sidewalks
and climbed up the crumbling steps.
knowing if i tripped you would catch me,
all worry banishing itself.
it's quiet now,
as if i'm overdosing on the drug you feed me
and i feed you.
the only sound left is breath
the only world left is ours
place?
time?
these moments go unrecorded.
that's what that kind of high will do to you.

ESCAPEE

Trapped in walls of concrete
Tinted panes of glass
Towers of darkness
Trees tap factory windows
Leaves paint shadow faces
Raindrops trace names
of previous prisoners
Flood water parts floorboards
Screaming souls wash away
Bodies of water
formed.

—Lucy Wilson

A B C

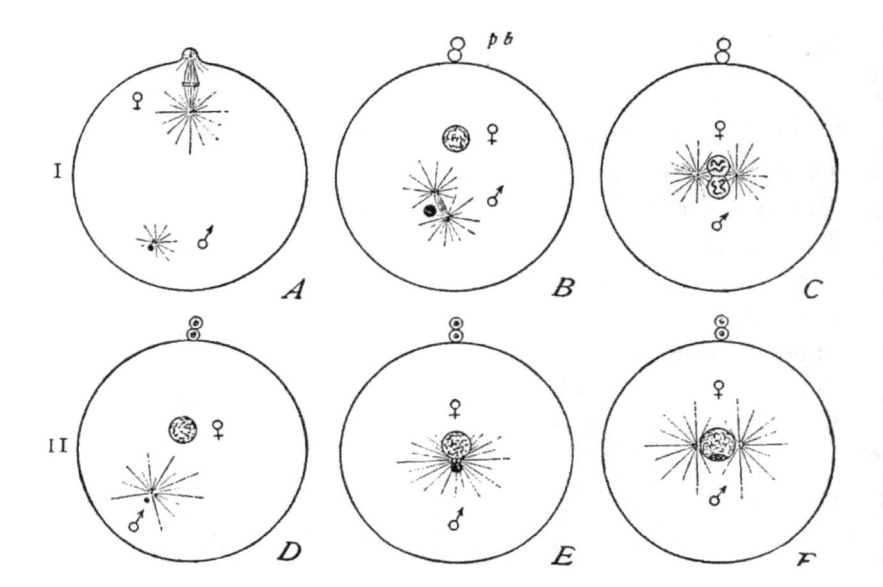

D E F

SKYE BOWDON

3 POEMS

ARSONIST

Bodies bleed sins,
eyes, ears, and mouth
fathers ask for autopsies.

My favorite color is lipstick
    Red.

The smell of lighter fluid is
    Nostalgic—

I strike matches in my room,
ode to the arsonist who creates
premature hell.

A kingdom of flame
engulfed
every love.

Ash is why
raven feathers are
    Black.

DECEPTION

you stand
in the mirror
motionless
stare forward

eyes
faded iris
eyes
tired and dry
they sting

straight
lips
lips cracked
and raw
pale painted rose

white shirt
black jeans
white and black
converse

in the long mirror

weak knees
you are irreparably
broken
china doll

useless
you are
unworthy
the nameless spirit
wither away

stolen
love
collapsing lungs
fail you
you are unlovable

tie tight
loose strings
fraying ends find
you

you are a reflection

SEEDS
A Pantoum

deity of poppies—
divine entity
    celestial fields
    raise into blue

divine entity
observe warmth and mild soil
raise into blue
and exist in scarlet

observe warmth and mild soil
    scatter me across ground
exist in scarlet
in ceremony

    scatter me across ground
    i'll root myself in ecstasy
    in ceremony
    nourished by rain

    i'll root myself in ecstasy
    blessed to be
    nourished by rain
    rest in the wind

    blessed to be
enlightened by silence
rest in the wind

...

    suspend me in forgetful bliss

enlightened by silence-
    celestial fields
    suspend me in forgetful bliss
deity of poppies.

—Skye Bowdon

DAKOTA ROSE

VANILLA TEARS

i.

Grandfather Sky looked down his pointed nose, the stormy, dark, clouds forming a frown.
For days on end, I was teased with the hopeful ease of rain.
Time dragged on, as my roots dried and leaves fell...
    Pitter patter
    Pitter patter
    Pitter patter
Lulling sounds of cool rain
Falling from the sky onto the leaves of my trees.
Fresh dew drops creep down my bark, sap and scents of vanilla.
Little bugs are swept away in the tidal wave of a single drop of rain.
    Pitter patter
    Pitter patter
The sweet teardrop of sky soaks the ground and joins its brothers and sisters
Darkening the soil, feeding the roots of trees, that vanilla scent.
    Pit
    Pit pat
    Pit
The rain slows,
The stories of Grandfather Sky's tears sink into the ground
Until they are embedded in me.
Earth and Sky are one.

ii.

I wake up and look out my window.
Through the gridded panels I see little white blankets
Resting on the needles of our history
Softening the spikes acquired through years
Of deforestation, blood and salty vanilla teardrop smiles
Snow covers the green pines as if to comfort them
I walk through the blizzard and stick out my tongue
Hoping a snowflake or two will find its way into my Earl Grey breath
I long for the taste of lingering tea and frozen vanilla
To mix and swirl on my tongue like the blizzard around me
I feel each individual snowflake
As they float onto my eyelashes
As I blink them into my peppered green eyes
Creating yet another identity.

iii.

I walk by windows in winter
    Do you often think of me?
The sun goes down and the snow shrouds the Earth
    Do you often taste my vanilla chapstick on your lips?
The temperature drops and slush turns to ice
    Do you often remember the late night chats
I walk by the doorways with lights all aglow
    and vanilla milkshake runs?
I walk by the cars, covered in a soft snow
    Do you often smell the sweet aroma of vanilla
I walk by the windows, warm lamplight seeps out
    perfume applied to the nape of my neck?
I see the families no longer out and about

> Do you often see lilies like I wore in my hair when we met?
> I scurry forward as my lips turn purple
> Do you often know I cry for you?
> I ball my hand, as the cold seeps into my metacarpal
> Do you often understand how I taste the salt of my tears
> Spinning around, I stick out my tongue
> mix with my vanilla chapstick
> Tasting the snow's stories of friends and music
> as they crawl down my face and onto my lips
> Of laughter and rum.
> all while I wish you would cry for me and my vanilla tears?

iv.

I think the world revolves around me.
My face says, *Don't mess with me*
People see me and say "She's very scary"
My heart says, *Listen to me!*
Hear my onomatopoeia
Sit with me and observe Cassiopeia.
Laugh and cry with me
Kiss the tears off my vanilla lips.
Pick me up and twirl me around,
all smiles and giggles and tummy butterflies
Taste the salty sweet of being right here—
> *With me.*

You don't think the world revolves around me.

—Dakota Rose

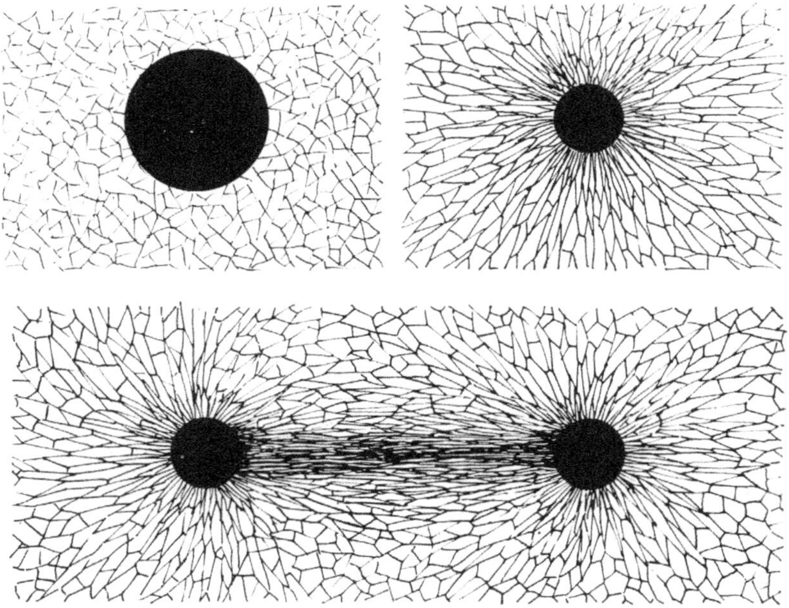

ANNABELLA HILL

NOVACAINE

Sometimes, you don't need some bad event for something to be wrong. Sometimes, you just need to wake up. Little things are much larger when you do. The plant dying on your windowsill seems like the end of the world. As you look at the withering leaves, your entire room feels wrong. Maybe you just have to work harder to see the light on those days, but sometimes your eyes are so filled with a dark static that you can't find the light.

That's how Constance saw it anyway. Even stars had to explode, sometime. Sometimes, they made beautiful, bright explosions that would be remembered for aeons. Others faded away, unseen. Constance wanted to be a beautiful star when she died. And maybe she would be, seeing as she was bound to one. A star that would die when she would. Constance often wondered if others were tied to stars too, and maybe they didn't know it. She looked out at the world, not sure what to think. There were so many beautiful things, but it was overwhelmed by the disgusting things destroying it. Her star would destroy *everything* when she died. She felt it would happen. Of course, she was paranoid about it, wondering when it would happen, if she had enough time to stop it, or if she should try to stop it.

Constance had another day of watching the world burn. She tried to see everything good, to convince herself that she needed to stop her star. It was getting harder, though. She looked out and saw people ignoring beauty, or killing it. The things they were hurting. Covering it up with false hopes, 'prayers', and sweets. Constance had taken a disliking to sweets, because no amount of candy could make everything okay. She sat on her couch, papers strewn about, pictures of beaches, forests, and people she found beautiful, charities, movements, and activists who tried to help. Tried to make everything okay, as sweets did not. The beautiful things and people were ignored. Constance had once ignored them, too. But she couldn't anymore, not when she knew the star that was to die with her would make the sky turn dark. If people were like her, they all had stars. Constance couldn't bear leaving the sky with no light to illuminate the pictures written within it.

She wasn't sure anymore, though. Some people, even if it wasn't all of them, were poison. They turned the rivers and forests black, making the sky turn gray and brown. They hid the pictures written out in the stars with their own arrogant light.

Dying plants and flowers lined her windows, fighting for sun, begging for a regular watering time. The city loomed outside, vast buildings casting shadows that stretched for miles. People bustled and struggled in cars and high heels, as if they were all going somewhere. Some went pointlessly, others went on with purpose. Constance took a deep breath of warm, stuffy air before joining them on the streets, her mind fogged. She wanted to move with a purpose, to make a decision. Should she really watch the sky go dark? Or should she save it?

Some people told her beautiful things. Those things gave her hope. These were little things most of the time, like sometimes a cat's eyes glow like burning candles to illuminate the night. An amber glow that cuts through the dark, leading you to some form of hope. Or that bees see flowers like little universes full of glowing stars. Bees collect those stars to make honey, Constance learned. Some things were larger, things that she discovered by herself.

Sometimes, if you were lucky, you'd meet someone who didn't

know how to hate. They lived in a world before god, before hatred existed. They lived in a time before god left them to figure out what hate was. She saw the universe in children's eyes, knick-knacks were treasures to them. They all had stories, true or false. If you listened to them enough, you would come across many of the universe's hidden secrets.

People glowed like cats' eyes, radiating like their stars that absorbed stories and memories. Constance found that if you stare at the night sky long enough, just like with objects, if you listen hard enough, it will tell you stories. People's stories dance across the sky on broken fingers of hardship and unanswered prayers. You pay for prayers in wishing wells with pennies, like children buying candy.

Constance strolled down the street, watching people, wondering how many of them bought the exact same prayer. They were strange like that. Maybe that's why she wanted to save them, so that they could have their prayer, and watch their stars flicker and dance across the night sky.

Constance liked to believe that everyone deserved to see their stars before they die out. Some people pushed her on that. Sometimes, she believed that these people couldn't possibly be people. Their poison was contagious. It spread like wildfire to others. How could they be people? Constance knew they were, deep down, but they were black holes, dying stars that fed on the emotional pain of others.

Ordering coffee, Constance sat down, wondering how you became a dying star. What would happen? How does the star inside of you die, the stardust in your body coming to a halt, the universe in your eyes going out like a light? Your veins no longer holding the same warmth, pulling people in with false hopes before you kill their star, too. It was a contagion everyone ignored, dying stars infecting the mind. They were hard to see sometimes, but always showed themselves sooner or later. Constance sipped her coffee thinking about the dying stars that dragged themselves to bars, sometimes forgetting why they took themselves out in the first place. They bought happiness and time on maxed-out credit cards, hoping they wouldn't turn into black holes. Constance figured everyone was scared of being a black hole, something that consumed light. You couldn't be fixed, then. Dying stars could be fixed, if you acted in time, sewing stardust back together with your veins, playing your best impression of a surgeon.

Everyone used their veins like thread to sew metals onto their skin, showing them to their stars, hoping one day to shine as brightly. Dying stars, made anew, were some of the most beautiful stars. Their wounds glowed like cats' eyes; their smiles were brilliant. Yet, their pain was real. It cut deep, but they didn't want others to feel the same thing. Leaving the coffee shop, she walked down the street, dodging between people, and waiting at crowded crosswalks. Families passed her, parents merely pretending to listen to their children. Should she try to change her star, or let it destroy the imperfect world? After all this time, she still wasn't sure. Not after all her travels. She had witnessed the beauty and poison in people, and both led her to different conclusions. However, only the tiny universes of flowers and the glowing embers of cats' eyes would tell her the answer. So far, they stayed silent. Stars were fickle like that. People bumped and pushed past her, hustling to their destinations. Would the sky be less beautiful if the stars went out? Or would it be more beautiful?

—Annabella Hill

SARITA GONZALEZ

4 POEMS

1939

I remember the first time I saw you
It was in a jazz club in Paris, France
I wore a brown suit and suspenders
to draw less attention

It took me just a bit too long to sit down
My cane was just barely holding my weight
The pain was almost unbearable
But as the room went dark
The pain faded away for once

The stage was lit
You stood there in a banana skirt
 and no top—
        Breathtaking—

With a sway of your hips
 the shine of your smile
You enthralled

As you flowed and skipped across the stage
You puckered your lips
crossed your eyes
pressed in your dimples
to laugh with us

You looked so joyful and free
A mix of childlike glee
And undeniable beauty
And then—
    You sang—

Soft enough to make me lean in
It was the bird song in the dead of night

And then
You were gone
    And I realized I hadn't touched
    my *Tequila con Limon*

You emerged from the stage door
And all I wanted to do was talk to you
Your voice was so much stronger in conversation
You asked about my cane
My life
And who I truly was

I finally understood our connection
When you told me about your pain
Your loss
About Harlem
And why you danced

We make art for the same reasons
You and I
Pain
That driving force

But we show it in different ways
You smile and dance
I cry and paint

Your heart glows with hope
And with a cracked soul
You bleed light
I knew I was talking with
A fellow goddess

We talked until sunrise
And when you left
All I could think was
    Josefine Baker y Frida Kahlo

It just sounds right.

ELEVEN

Eleven women buried on the West Mesa
Eleven souls forgotten by Burque
Eleven women that had their breath stolen away
because of the life they were forced to live
How did we let this happen?
Broken
Broken society forcing people into an idea
that's not possible
Making them hide
in something that is broken
Until it crumbles on top
and all around them
They were Burque's most vulnerable
Why do we look the other way
when these people vanish
again
and again
and again
Even though it is us that forced them into this life
because they did not fit in?
They were once innocent children
that fell into the hole society dug
And we were the ones that buried them
They were women with nowhere to go
Because of us

Jamie, 15
Monica, 22
Victoria, 26
Virginia, 24

Syllania, 15
Cinnamon, 32
Doreen, 24
Julie, 24
Veronica, 28
Evelyn, 27
Michelle, 22

Michelle's unborn baby, 4 months in utero
All women of color
All turned away
All gone
Consumed by society's wrath
The dust of their bodies
becoming the dust on shelves
Forgotten
Buried near the prayers in rock written by ancestors
Their only protection
The petroglyphs
Why did society just ignore these women?
Our women are dying
Their lives have become
of no value
So now
we have a choice
We can gather all of our sisters
like a pack of *lobas*
Howl at the moon
And make it clear
That we are not going to stay silent
anymore
Or we can do what they want us to do
And pretend it never happened

. . .

If we don't stand for ourselves now
Women will continue to be disrespected
Taken advantage of
And the cycle will continue
within each generation
Let us become one
Take a stand
And never forget these lives
that were stolen
We must evolve
Into a new culture
of women and community
Help save our own.

IVORY 505

When I walk down the drugstore makeup aisle
I look for
CoverGirl Clean Matte pressed powder shade *Ivory 505*
the lightest shade they make
My grandma looks for *Classic Tan 450*
a Sunkissed golden tone
My mom looks for *Buff Beige 125*
a warm peach tone
Yet I am still the most *güera* with
Ivory 505
Since I was little
Mi Familia has called me *Güerita*
Little girl
With golden curls
Hazel eyes
Light skin
It is meant to be a term of endearment
But some of us *güeras*
are starting to get a complex
Feeling like an outcast with my own *gente*
Stumbling over my tongue just to talk with my *abuelita*
Constantly having my authenticity questioned
Trying to prove that I am just as *Chicana* as they come
I was born and raised in the 505
A place where my community thrives, lives, and loves
A place where the Sandía mountains
Rise out of the ground as if Mother Earth was reaching up to grab
our *Zia* Sun
The 505
where white sand dunes glitter and shimmer like snow in the moonlight

. . .

lighter than the sand on the banks of the *Bosque*
but it is still New Mexico *tierra*
Just like the dark brown sand from *Santuario de Chimayo* that heals
and protects my soul
The 505
where the powerful current of the *Rio Grande* flows through
and heals my heart
she sings to me
I know all of her songs
holding my culture close
Every step I make I'm dancing to a *Cumbia*
Every breath I take is a prayer to *La Virgen*
Every word I say has a hint of Spanglish
My heart tries to sing *boleros* at midnight
My ears are always listening for *chisme*
I can take *carilla* from *mi familia*
And yet to some, I am still not *Chicana* enough
Sometimes I feel just like Abraham Quitania:
"We have to be more Mexican than the Mexicans, and more American than the Americans, both at the same time! It's exhausting!"

I am tired of running this marathon
I am tired of jumping through hoops
I am tired of trying to fit in your mold

My Spanish will always be on the *pocho* side
My tortillas will never be perfectly round
My looks will never be that of an Aztec princess
But my love for *mi cultura* will never fade
And this *Chicana* still carries her *Ivory 505* compact in her back pocket.

SAVE

A mother can only hold it in for it in for so long before the dam breaks
A wife can only stay strong until the current rips her away
I wasn't able to save you
they turned us away
no help
The only way to save you
we bring you over
Children and Families are torn apart
I can't leave you
Sunburnt and broken
The only option is
trust *el Rio Grande's* strength
She can boil, freeze, and drown you
But if there's a chance for your future
We must take it
Time is deconstructed by the current
Your Father will try to make a deal with the river for you
I lift you up onto your father's back
The water rushes with the melting snow
He slowly slides into the water
He trudged through
With your feet just barely touching the cold brown river
I finally feel hope again
Hope that you will be safe
Just as safe as when you were in my womb
Protected by *familia* and kept warm by *mi Corazon*
Hope that I can watch you graduate
To see you get an education
And go on to do better things
Hope that I will grow old with your father

...

Have a man to stand by my side with no regret and no amount of
    selfishness
Until we pass on to become the spirits to protect you
Only have to cross this river
And we will truly be okay
All of that is gone in a moment of pure pain
In an instant she took you both
I tried to chase the river
But the flow of her power was too fast
I screamed and cried out in pain
Calling for you and your father
Screaming to hold you and see you
Panicking trying to make sure you're okay
Calling for help
Help at the border line for people that wouldn't find us
Help that they wouldn't even give us when we were right in front
    of their faces
Calling for freedom
Wanting to be in a place that I thought would be safer
I searched and searched for you until you washed up
You held him so tightly until Your
final breath.

—*Sarita Gonzalez*

MYLIE JONES

THE LAST GLASS

Scoria sat on a tilted aurora spire, one of many sticking out of the diamond sand that expanded wide, in endless directions, beneath the sky. Colors danced through their body, reflecting in vivid volcanic swirls behind them. They let their eyes blur the world, turning it into a stained-glass window. Their mouth gaped to breathe the air, bubbles of red heat cooling and stilling, trapped in eternity beneath translucent skin. Beaded quartz tears rippled down their cheeks, an escapade of burning trails where the drops fell. The bubbles made Scoria restless, so they stood on the sharp end of the spire to face the sun, dye and water blending as their feet sank into the tip. *Clink, clink...* Footsteps floated along the path from the gleaming palace in the background. Scoria turned around, glistening light across their bare back. They tapped down the spire to meet Spume, touching feet down to meet spicule glass.

Clink. "Why do you cry?" *Clink, clink.*

"I cry for Bumble. Did you not hear, Spume?" The clinks froze, icy lake eyes stabbed Scoria through. A frown, a grimace, crossed arms.

"I heard. It is nothing to cry for. Shatters happen. Bumble can be fixed. You have too much empathy. You'll make Nocturne's job harder by ruining your face with those tears." Spume crossed to Scoria, tidal waves crashing against glass, magnifying the sun and sending blue to the sand. They caressed Scoria's face with a soft tap. An ocean clone looking to through the eyes of their lava sibling.

Scoria drew away, touching their hand to Spume's. They didn't agree with the words Spume spoke. It was true that Bumble could be returned to their former self, but the cracks would remain. The trauma which shattered them would return lost memories and changes to personality. Bumble would be clouded, fogged by the frozen chills of their destruction. Scoria cried for the cracks, the pieces that could never be returned. Spume wouldn't understand this. Bumble's breakage was acceptable, since they could be returned. Their species were not creatures of flesh and bone, whose spirit left after their brains were deprived of the delicate balance of their bodies. There was no need for concern.

"You are correct. I do not know why I cry. I shall stop, so I do not create more work for Nocturne." Spume nodded, a smile melting on their lips, moving their hand once again to tap against Scoria's face. They drew Scoria into a hug, fingers running through the fluid strands of window that ran down Scoria's back. Unfinished dolls clinging together. Sick comfort against Scoria's shoulder blade. Deep ocean chill running down Scoria's spine. There was nothing to grieve. Grief was not fair to those who had processed the trauma of breakage and continued on. Tears would only create more negative presence, more cracks in their skin. Less room for the colors to dance through when they sat in the warm sunlight.

Scoria stepped back from Spume's arms, retreating across the reflective sand to touch their boiling back against the spire. "You must have come for a reason. What might I help you with?"

Spume stepped forward, blue stirring with red and rainbow, their gaze hard pebbles against Scoria's eyes. Scoria shrunk, their eyes darting down to escape Spume's. They wandered across the tall, stained-glass buildings in the distance, reflecting prismatic rays of light, down to their feet, lava bubbling up from their toes from small, brown landscapes at the tips. "A moth."

Scoria tilted their head, glass brow folding in on itself. "A moth?"

"Yes. A moth. That's what happened to Bumble." Spume placed their hands upon Scoria's shoulder. They were insistent on physical contact, a needy wolf.

Scoria couldn't fathom Spume's need to place themself in the alpha position, dominating through false kindness. They wanted only to control. In truth, Spume wasn't the glass people's leader, they only played at it. Scoria's magma brain couldn't process what "a moth" meant. "I don't understand what you mean. You must go into more detail." Moths existed, small insects with vintage rum-bottle wings and clouded sea-glass bodies. They fluttered around and nibbled at brethren materials, though one could usually bat them before they did any damage. Annoying, but with Spume's oozing voice, the moths were sounding sinister.

"There is one strange, disturbing thing about Bumble's breakage. Fluorescence reported a new species of moth upon Bumble's head. The moth touched Bumble for but a moment, but once it did, its wings became a colorful, painted glass and it shone anew. Its body thinned, its wings spread, and it fluttered. Then, gone! Out an open window." Spume's eyes were wide, fingers dancing on Scoria's shoulders as if they were attempting to spark a terrified tingle. "This was right before Bumble took a hard glass rock... *and smashed themselves in!*"

This last sentence sent spiders crawling along Scoria's surface. Sand crunched beneath Scoria's feet as they forced themselves past Spume without a word.

Spume called after Scoria in their frustrated alpha voice.

Scoria broke into a run, grainy shards softening and melting under their flying feet. The spire cast an echo after them, sad to be left by their faithful company, but Scoria had to make their way to Bumble.

Scoria came to the Great Palace, spires at the top of every roof, a colorfield of luminous glass. They imagined this was what the moth had looked like. The building where they lived poked its way into view. Scoria halted outside its door. They shoved it open, upon a bustling commonplace of glassy beings, each form made of beautiful, solid colors they had never seen before. The room was spacious, bright rays shining through the glass and casting the room in a blinding lace.

Scoria pushed through the people, their body clinking against others as they fought the current. To Nocturne…They had to get to where Nocturne worked. Bumble should be together soon, a whole piece, though a piece with little bits of themselves gone, and a nightmare hatching in their surface. Scoria felt awful for that, like the little lava flows inside them were burning through, casting the world in a hot fire of desolation. It only worsened when Scoria didn't cry. Nocturne would be concerned. There would be disappointment, more of it, and a warning that they must bottle things inside. Showing emotion led to breakages. Showing emotion led to death. Emotions were too great for their fragile glass bodies, emotions were gathering inside, and the bubbles had to explode to be released, as they were cold and would only sink to their feet otherwise.

Scoria climbed a rippling staircase, the glass beneath their feet soft and moldable against their toes. They hopped up each step, hovering like a hummingbird. Up and up, far above everything, away from the noise, close to where the sun spread its warmth, a heaven for the unwell.

Scoria hit the third-to-top step.

Scraping metal, a knife scraping against a metal bottle ricketing against Scoria's ears, filling the upper halls.

Scoria hesitated.

Someone's screams, a horrendous cacophony of the most unpleasant of noises, a nail along glass, the wail of a small child, the cry of a peacock, piling together in a single voice.

Such pain and struggle that had never been heard by any glass person.

Scoria stepped against the crystalline floor, glass fingers clicking as their hands quaked, and the shrieking continued without pause. No desperate gasp for air, no fading into sobs, only the never-ending cry.

Scoria's head felt as if it were cracking, as if the noise itself was scratching canyons into their skin, branching from the inside of their skull. They made their way to the infirmary with teetering steps, creaking down the hall.

Their body jerked back, lava bubbles spiraling and shaking, unrest within the cold pocket of their stomach. A new sensation of utter despair and hopeless curls clawing within them. Physical pain wracked up to accompany these feelings, crashing within them, screams and more screams.

Colonies of shattered glass surrounded by leaves, rocks, other objects, living creatures. Glass crawling with alien things that had escaped the barriers. Scoria stared at the scene with glazed pupils, the lava within them flowing from the rocks beneath their skin and blistering, making their transparency opaque.

Scoria's emotions teetered at the edge of the table and fell, spilling their contents as the container stabbed into the blood and flesh they would never know.

Forward, continue forward.

The canyons were extending.

Lava was milking to the floor, burning through and dripping through to cause damage and panic to those beneath.

Scoria, without an arm, on their hands and knees, crawled in a bleeding desperation to the doorway, where the horrendous cry originated.

There was a murmuring beneath, buzzing from the walls in a broken vibration, whispering. It was alright. It was permissible to cry, the pain was true. It alone was real. Keep feeling, keep feeling. Their feelings had been caged too long. The whispers became separate, opinions separating but surrounding the release of their budding expressions. The rasps drowning in the grating. The voices on the walls were an artwork of fragile wings, dye spreading across them in disorganized splatters. Painted glass butterflies with wings each the size of Scoria's hand, string bodies as long as their middle finger. The insects fluttered, vibrations of voice from their wings.

Scoria's was lost once again, blind, searching, finding their way to the source of the unbearable screeching. In a corner, Bumble was fixed. Scattered shards of Nocturne and Nocturne's helpers lay in a spread across the floor, their insides crawling across the glass in a living mass of liquid and creature.

Scoria collapsed. Their remaining arm ran to pieces to join the others, and they stared at Bumble with the salty fissures in their cheeks flooding.

Bumble was clouded, their glass filled with a swirling mist which flowed out from the holes alongside the few remaining bees, going to join the whispering butterflies.

Scoria wanted to reach out, to comfort Bumble. Pain pounded through the room, heavy. The pain broke them. The pain had shattered the rest. And now Scoria, too, would be shattered by the pain. Scoria's chest beat. The rhythm that filled the room. A music that was built by a scraping caterwaul and hoarse words, kept in a woven basket by the heartbeat of crucifixion.

A group of butterflies lifted, their wings fluttering in rhythm.

A true song.

Scoria was focused on Bumble, Bumble who was surrounded by shards of those their cry had brought to an end.

But Bumble's wail never paused.

Bumble's eyes were lost to Scoria, but Scoria added their own murmuring to the song. They wanted to be a part of the music. A simple murmur of Bumble's name.

Scoria's body went in an upsurge.

It jumped and was carried and melted by the lava that remained, a tide that sent Scoria into a melting ocean.

The song buzzed on.

Bumble's cry grew louder, the vibrations lengthened.

The song made its way to creep down the stairs.

The butterflies took flight.

The glass grained.

The light shone through wings and cracked lifeforms.

The frozen still life of an eternal shriek and the color stuck to the walls.

—Mylie Jones

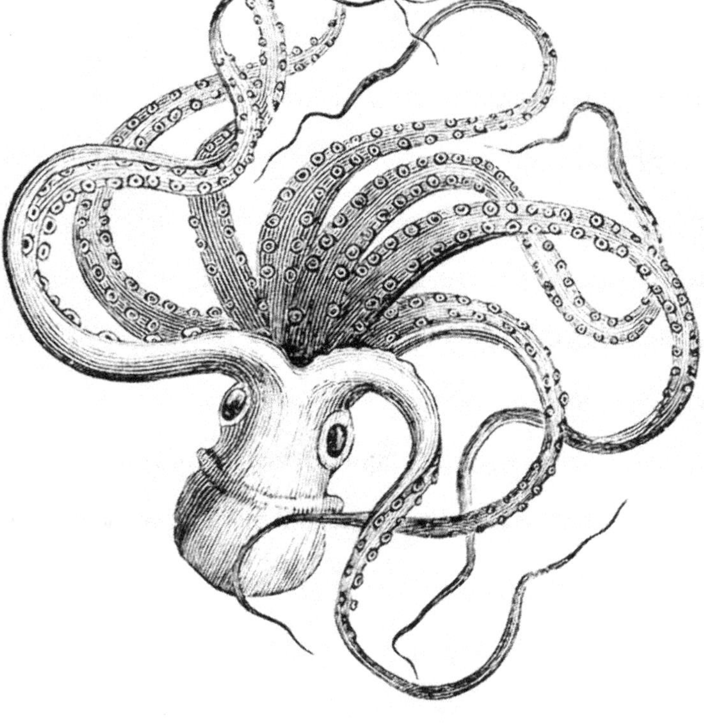

ISABELLA FLETCHER

2 POEMS

MELANCHOLY

A deep red
Inflamed like a mosquito bite
He drinks color from my lips
Smells like fresh metal

My head clenched as a fist
But he spread and scurried
Around my skull
Melting down
Pulsing violet veins

He capsules my chest
Robs my lungs of air
Between each muscle
And the streaming blood
He squeezes
My pumping heart

He struck in my core, but
I absorb him like a sponge
He soaks into my flesh
He holds tight to my bones

Now, now, now
In the center of my stomach
He swirls like a tornado
Grips my soul
I suffocate

And yet, I let him
Rise through my spine
pour out my salted eyes
He sits   Waiting
Brewing like a storm

STOLEN

Look into the eyes of a woman
Weeping for what she could not give
Stolen like precious rubies from her womb

Red as the blood
That stains her cheeks
From tearing

Look into the eyes of a man
Who seeks power, control
Cold is the soul who takes the light

The stolen light of her eyes
With the prohibition of her right
Her voice, because he's afraid of it

Look into the eyes of a trembling child
Whose tiny body will never know the warm embrace
Of a mother

Stolen are the child's nights
She stays awake wondering
Why she wasn't wanted

Stolen
She will never know
She was stolen

—Isabella Fletcher

Ps

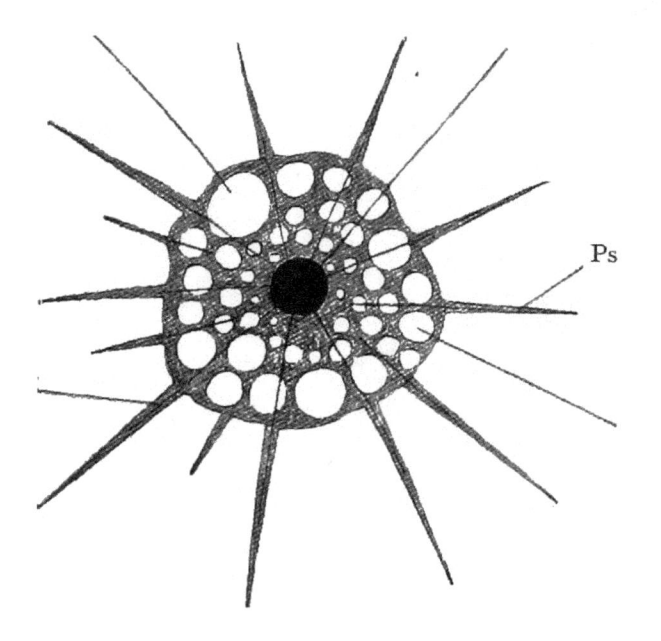

LUCIA ROSEN

WE TOOK FLIGHT

i.

We grew up understanding why we had to take our shoes off and put our computers in bins as we walked through radiated scans. We understood why, when we would accidentally push the exit door, loud, obnoxious alarms went off. We would go cry into our mom's arms apologizing to anyone and everyone who had to hear that horrifying noise. Every time we would see one of those doors, we would try to sit as far away as we possibly could, but close enough to see the airplanes take off. That trauma would be engraved into our lives.

ii.

9/11. 3 days after the most important day of my uncle's life. 3,000 people killed for the entertainment of Osama Bin Laden. That moment was overwhelming. Every news screen, radio broadcast, and newspaper headline projected the terrors of the massacre. People were closed up in their houses. They hid under their covers with their eyes pinned shut, so they could get lost in their dreams of a better life, and happiness. The life that held their greatest desires, hopes, aspirations, and love. But, when they opened their eyes, they saw screaming children blackened with a cloud of sadness, buildings that once held the future of our economy, now burning a hole into middle-class pockets, and families taken from one another.

iii.

BREAKING NEWS: KOBE BRYANT AND DAUGHTER, 13, DEAD IN HELICOPTER CRASH. Number 24. The legend that made me want to become a basketball player when I was 8. Every time I threw a piece of loose leaf with tears stained into the ink I would yell "KOBE!" The legend that made me want to work hard and not have any excuses for my success. The legend that made me believe in believing that dreams do come true. He made me believe that hard work does pay off. However, one-day people will stop remembering the headline that made the world silent. The heart-wrenching incident that made everyone wonder why bad things happen to good people. The misfortune of the loss of a rapist. One man that brought so much good into the world, but got away with so much evil. No one will ever talk about that.

iv.

FEAR: an unpleasant emotion caused by the belief that someone, or something, is dangerously likely to cause pain, or a threat. What about being afraid to go on stage? Or having fears for your future? Not knowing what is to come. That's fear too right? There is so much that can happen, but this fear, with its negative connotations, can be turned into a positive emotion. The fear of success. Do people fear success? Why?

v.

When the towers came crashing down, the world shook with fear. Ever since that jaw-dropping moment, America has been living in fear. The fear of never knowing what is going to happen, or the last time you will see someone. That day is always replaying and always in the back of my mind. It made me realize that bad things happen to good people. The knowledge that someone I hold so dear in my heart can be taken away so easily within seconds. There is so much evil in the world that it has made so many people heartless. Nobody has sympathy, anymore. The hate has taken over.

vi.

My life has been filled with fear. The fear of my school getting shot up. The fear that our airplane might crash. The fear that I will break my leg skiing. The fear that my parents might die in a car accident. That fear is one of my biggest regrets. The regret that I can never just be in the present, and explore this mystery called life. My dad raised me to live with no regrets, and to learn from things, always. However, I am constantly regretting one little thing I say to a friend, or I can't let go of discomfort if I hugged someone weirdly, three days earlier. Now, these aren't huge fears or even fears, at all, but they scare me. I don't want to live with regrets, but they are always coming up in my life.

—Lucia Rosen

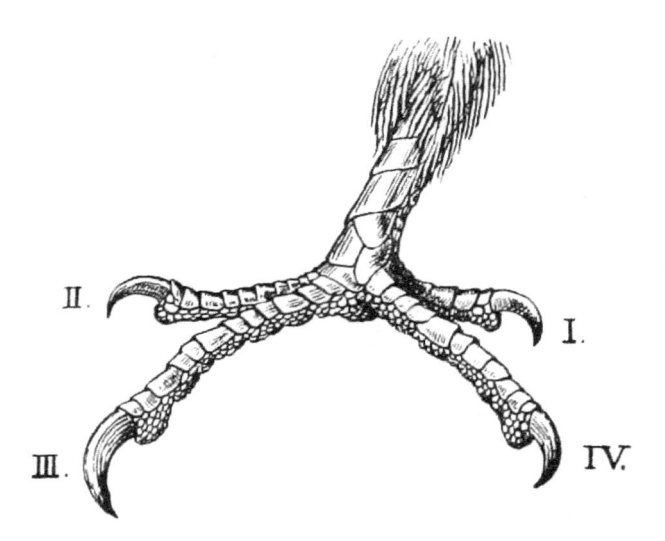

II.   I.

III.   IV.

SEAN MONTOYA

BLAME

I think my mouth
Is my worst enemy.
The same mouth that allows the toxins
To riddle my body
And break down my shape.
My mouth can surprise and
Let beauty escape
Though, the beauty is rare and crass
Is it even beauty at all?

>
> You speak of beauty
> With no specifics,
> Yet, expect me to bore
> All the same?
> I am not a gimmick.
> You can launch your quarters
> Into my taverns,
> But do not expect
> Tastes like that of gumballs
> in my words.

My mouth.
It infects my life
And smells of death
With the corpses that lie inside.
The bodies are plaqued and brittle
With roots that sink into
The cave that bleeds and gorges sorely
On dwindling smiles is followed
By scrunching torsos.

>Yes, corpses hath
>Become my integrity,
>But is it not you who commit the crime?
>You are the hammer and chisel
>That ignores all stamps of time.
>The ground below you withers
>And yet
>You take its nutrients
>And crash more of your cars
>All for the sake of proving
>you are the masters.

Yes.
My mouth is someone I truly hate.
Hate for the yellow and stain
That imprints in eyes
And speaks of horror at which I cannot laugh.
I've spoken with those bones
I have
They hug too tight
With fear of losing each other
In the thrashing tides

I ask why!
Acknowledge my voice
and not only my name!
You illustrate my troubles
And list them as your own!
Your fears and pain grow far beyond
What I supposedly cause you.
Until you can face that you are to blame
Please just accept that we are the same.

—Sean Montoya

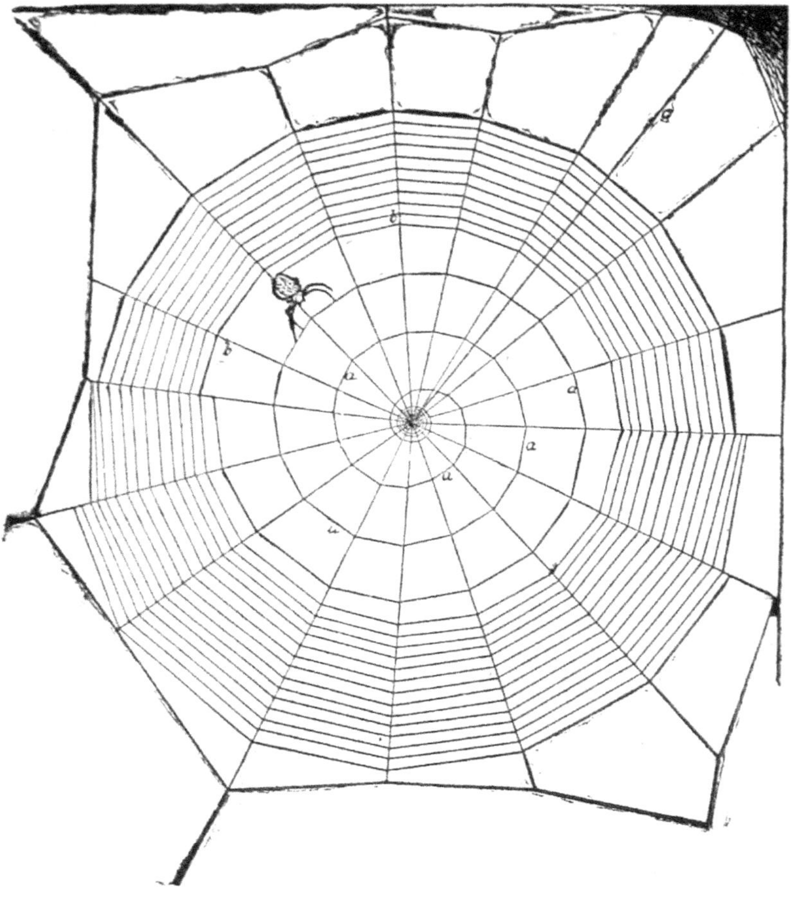
b
b
a
a
a
a
a

ADRIENNE RUGG

FOUR POEMS

INCUBUS

Two girls stand across a parking lot
One dressed in black
One dressed in white.
The rain pounds down onto the asphalt
So hard that their faces are blurred through the distance.
If they even had faces
They would be the fragments of my long-lost lovers —
The ones I'm not guilty to forget.
My clothes are weighted with water.
This ring of champagne-gray Mercedes,
Empty
With the passenger-side doors open to the harsh rain,
Separate us.
But the space does not dull the creeping dread.
They are holding hands.
These are the children of the incubus. This is what
Springs forth, foaming and raving from the stark depths
Of my fear. This is what comes when the
Gods are gone.
Before I sleep I listen to music that I can't understand
The lyrics whisper strange promises

...

That someday we will all be ashen remnants
And that is payment enough.
There are still two girls standing in the rain.
It's the dreadful clenching panic in my heart
Of drowning eternally in the deep
Rain.
Last year I drowned for three weeks
And I only cried twice.

FEAR OF FALLING

Remember your burning flesh in the haunting fires of fall
The smell of fresh roasted chiles
And red lilies with their lips dyed in blood.
You are trapped on a stage for all your burning life.
Emergency exits glow red
To your right.
Falling leaves and flat notes on pianos
As out of tune as the drumbeats in your head.
Your heart beats in your head.
You beat your head against the emergency exit,
Tinted glass beats back with the haunting fires of a wet summer
Until you pass into the burning lilies,
Lips died in red.

THE MOTH

I am a little eyeball with feet
I am a tale of watermelons
I am a newly cut leaf
I am a sundog
I am a noise in the engine
I am an ice cube in the ocean
I am a deep-dish apple pie
I am the cracks on the screen
I am a painful green dot on the carpet
I am the English language
I am a prospective photograph
I am a feathered panther
I am the last-minute cancellations on a Tuesday afternoon
I am a trail of ants
I am the low-frequency chirping
I am the redshirted old man
I am a hungry moth at the porchlight
I am a printer running out of ink.

IN WAR

You fight for your honor.
You fight for your country. Our country.
You are like a beast of battle and
You are the one prophesied by the great gods of times long past.
You are the only one who can tell the story after every other soldier
    is dead.
You are the one who can win this but you must do it alone and
I cannot give you that.
You hear the wailing of the jungle and the rush of blood
You smell death everywhere, don't you? It surrounds you in the
    warzone.
You are all alone, about to die in the wailing jungle
You long for something like safety, love, home, and
I am sorry but
I cannot give you that.
You will be out there in the wild after your companions tell you to
    run.
You will save yourself and no one will come with you.
You will be alone and the battle will be over.
You will become part of the trees and vines
You will live in a cave and learn to live with the blind apes
    surrounding you
You will drink your own tears when you run out of water.

—Adrienne Rugg

GIOVANNA KALANGIS

BLURRED

Gunshots shatter the silence and draw a shriek of terror from her lips. It is 4:00 a.m., on the morning of her birthday, and below her family's apartment, down on the street, she hears the alarmed voices of children. She has stopped counting the number of riots that have taken place in her town over the past year, but she knows the number is well over one hundred. The noise continues for hours. The sound of chanting and screaming never stops, and neither does the sporadic gunfire. She gets ready for school three hours early out of pure anxiety. School has not been cancelled, which is no surprise. The riots are normal, now. She mentally prepares herself to cross the river of protesters outside of her house. As she puts on her backpack, her mother reminds her, yet again, that it is better to hide among them, and cross *slowly*, than to run. "Blend in, my love. You never know who is watching. Running draws attention, and the gunmen will target anyone who does not blend in." The girl rolls her eyes. This is probably the thousandth time she has heard this. But she doesn't have the heart to tell her mother that she is used to being scared.

She slips out of the door, closing it softly behind her and snaking discreetly into the crowd. She pushes and pivots, sneaks and stumbles through the protesters until she makes it to the other side of the street, where she begins her two-mile trek to the nearest school. Three policemen stop her along the way and ask where she is going. Sometimes she lies and says that she is going to deliver supplies to her sickly aunt. They do not have time to search her, and she is grateful.

School is long and drags. Too many times, a knock comes at the tiny classroom's door, and military men come in to check backpacks for weapons. They are gruff and angry, all of them wishing they were somewhere else, wishing they weren't trapped in this like the others. At least they get to pretend, but honestly, she sometimes thinks they have it worse than the rest of them.

The walk home is strangely free of military policemen. No trucks full of soldiers pass by, and no one searches her. She is not even stopped for a moment. No one pays her any attention. She reaches her apartment building and makes her way up the four flights of ugly, unpainted concrete stairs to her home, expecting to see her mother waiting for her in the living room. But as she opens the squeaky door, it reveals an empty room and the sound of urgent voices coming from her parents' bedroom. She calls out, and her mother comes rushing out of the back room, hoisting a gigantic suitcase awkwardly over one shoulder, her face flushed and sweating. Her mother tells her to put all the belongings that she cares about into her school backpack and her duffel bag. "We're leaving, before this entire wretched place burns!" The girl does not ask questions, packing her pants and shirts into her duffel. She is tempted to bring her birthday party dress, but thinks better of it.

A half hour later, she has escaped the house along with her parents, holding only her clothes, her flip phone, and her teddy bear across her back. She is wearing a life jacket over her clothing, even though they are hours away by car from the nearest Turkish port. It's hot, and all she can think about is taking it off. Her mother says there will not be time to put it on when they get there. "Everything will look too blurry anyway."

The next day, a sinister-looking man loads them onto a small inflatable boat along with fifty-two others, refusing to look any of them in the eye. She seems to have forgotten where she put her life jacket from home. Her mother was right, everything is too blurry to remember. The man hands her a replacement and she is too scared to ask him what they are made of. She has heard so many rumors. Some say the life jackets are made of Styrofoam, and some say they are made of the souls of dead children.

✷

Later, a toddler falls into the water.

✷

He does not float back up for a long time. His mother is screaming, tearing at her hijab, revealing the sable black of her hair. But here, no one cares about her hijab. When he resurfaces, his beautiful baby skin is bloated and blue. He looks like plastic. The girl looks away and vomits over the side.

As she looks into the deep, gloomy blue-black of the sea, and gazes at her own murky eyes reflected in the water, something seems different, in the way that everything is now. She recognizes nothing about herself. It is easier to pretend she never even existed. The waves could be beautiful and serene, but the girl senses that they are against her. After three hours of staring blankly at them, she closes her eyes and leans against her father. She tries to think about what birthday presents she might have gotten if she was home.

✷

Thirteen more people fall into the water before they reach land. Ten of them don't survive. The bodies are left in the water. They weigh too much to pull back onto the boat. They remain face down, almost peaceful.

The smells of the salt water and sweat fill her nostrils. The swell gives her a headache and makes her seasickness worse. The water seems like a never-ending poison. She hates it. It reminds her of the impermanence of home. Even in her early childhood, she understood that water is serious. It has a presence, deep, dark and soulful. A wicked beauty, too easy to become trapped in.

*

When they reach the island, there is no one waiting for them. Not a soul stands among the rocks on the beach to wave in welcome. They are utterly alone.

*

They walk for two days.

*

They stop at a tiny gas station to buy a bottle of water and some bread. The man behind the counter glares and yells something that no one understands. The price tags exhibit lower prices than he charges her father. But they are desperate, so they do not ask. The girl takes note that they only have eight euros left.

Twelve miles away from the main town on the island, they see hundreds of people. Hundreds of people like them. People fleeing their homes and lives. Women push strollers and hold the hands of their children. Teenage boys walk in huddles to the nearest grocery store, counting their money as though they are obsessed, their hands twitching at their pockets as if it will disappear any minute. No one smiles. No one laughs.

*

When they get to the camp site, the girl is separated from her parents and put into a small tent with fourteen other girls. They are not scared anymore. They say you must have hope to be scared. They do not have the privilege of hope, they say. It is too risky.

*

A week later, she finds a lighter. When she sets fire to the tent, no one protests. When it begins to spread across the camp in a circling halo of sparks and smoke, no one flees, for they have no more life to live. She holds a makeshift torch made of her hijab and some gasoline up in the air like a prayer, until it blisters and burns her hand, but she does not let go. She screams. She screams for justice, for pain, for love, for hatred. But she does not let go.

—Giovanna Kalangis

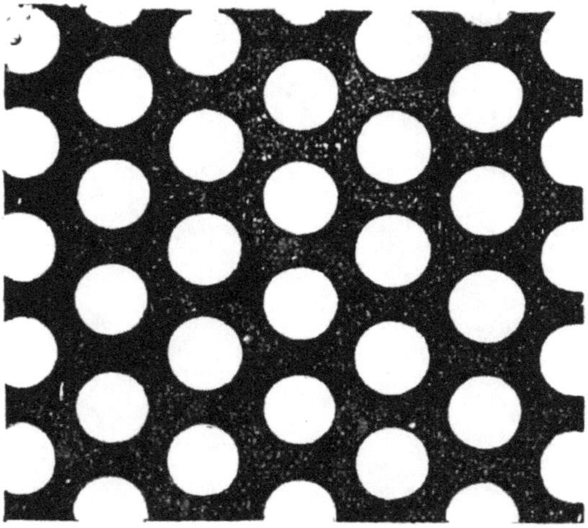

PEARL COOK

127

music plays
in my head
    Repeat

i listen to music
with my head underwater
drowning out my thoughts
              Right?
    Repeat

waves come
crashing down
    Repeat

water floods my ears
memories cave my head
    Repeat

voice above
don't listen
    Repeat

where are you?
will they listen?
can this help me?
    Repeat

can you answer
my simple question
drowning out my thoughts
              Right?
    Repeat

—Pearl Cook

ANNABELLA HILL

THE DOLL KINGDOM

Chantilly didn't know how, or why, she was there. Trapped in a gown that squeezed and formed her waist into an hourglass, ticking down the seconds. Wallpaper laced in gold, dripping with velvety floral designs and stretched tightly over the plaster like skin. She strolled through the labyrinth. Faces loomed over her, smiling down. Blank eyes watched her every move. Humming resounded through the corridors, like hundreds of bees tripping and tumbling over the waterfall of lace and cloth. Chantilly gripped her head, pace quickening, the sound of her heels clacking. A waltz sounded through the halls and echoed within her. Figures danced at the corners of her vision. Dolls, scooping her up, pulled Chantilly into step with them. She didn't know the rhythm. It changed, weaving in and out of symphonies. Painted smiles swept through her. Ball-joints cracked and splintered into place while they passed her through the crowd. The walls stretched and grew. Budding flowers ruptured out of the skin, gnarled roots twisted out of the thin paper, and thorns ripped and clawed the ground. The dolls skipped over them, and warm golden light washed through their painted faces.

Crescent moons floated through the dancehall, snatched up by swallows, pulling her relentlessly, returning her always to the dance. The golden light revealed a forest of peeling skin wallpaper, stitching itself back together with thorns. The humming turned into a quiet scream, the dolls staring at her from the doorway looking down at her from the ceiling. They hung on thin wires, that threatened to snap, as their waltz continued. Swallows plucked at her hair and clothes, painting them in the crescent moons and stars that cut through the blue-black blanket of the dancehall. Chantilly ran, smacking into the paper. The thorns tore at her dress and her white skin. Time flooded the dolls. Chantilly watched them rot and fall apart, paint chipping and peeling off. Maggots and beetles crawled through the soft woodflesh. Yet, new dolls replaced them, with new paint, new garb. Always, they dragged her back in.

She had to know what they were. What made them? Why was she here with them?

At last, she struggled into another room. Red thread twisted around her bones. She tripped over her feet. She was terrified of this dance. The dolls stared. The eyes, they never stopped. They anchored her to the ground, and once more, the dolls passed her through the room. Each spun her around before the thread bound them together. She was passed on. They were the dolls, but she was the toy. Given to one after the next, time slowed now to a painful crawl. Each second felt like a year, but the hall was never quite still. They never stopped pulling and twisting, never stopped their slow screaming. She struggled, trying to break free of the dance. It got faster, louder again. She stumbled over her feet, and squeezed her eyes shut.

It stopped.

Chantilly couldn't tell what had happened. When she opened her eyes, all that remained in place of the dancehall was a desolate labyrinth of tombs. Doll bodies rotted and piled in the rooms, wood splintered and decomposing into the floors. She walked where the labyrinth had been. The silence pressed the air from her lungs. She gasped and picked up her feet, stepping over the bodies. She tried not to touch them and their rot. Their peeling faces stared up at her, their fading whispers working into her head. They begged her to step on them, erase the last pains, and all that they had been.

They burst into a horrible, shattering laughter. Chantilly gripped her head and inhaled sharp breaths. The laughter invaded her mind, ringing through its rooms. She stumbled, trying to get it out of her head. She needed to get the voices out. They had to get out! She shook her head, trying to cast them out, threads twisting her bones until she heard a crack...

...Then silence.

A glance down and she saw a doll's face, shattered like glass under her foot, decaying paint stuck to the bottom of her shoe. Insects scrambled along her socks, against the frozen, pale skin of her legs. She could only muster an aching groan of horror, her throat constricting. She had stepped on one. Dear God, she stepped on one! Webs of pain shot through her. She screamed, clawing at it. Blood seeped from her paper skin. With the blood, maggots erupted. She tried to wipe them away, to get them off. The wretched bugs broke and writhed from her peeling wax. Her scream shattered the rest of the dolls' bodies like exploding windows. Tears of glass rained from the sky, pinning anything that moved to the ground. Writhing puss flowed from her waxen paper, peeling it back with fire and needles. Rivers flowed from her face, crystals caught in her eyes, forcing her to see double before the black-headed demons ceased.

"Please, please why am I here? God I just want to leave!" she shrieked to the silence, choking back her tears, and using her dirty sleeve to wipe them away. She crumpled to her knees, wiping blood from her leg, but finding no wounds. All that remained was red skin, as if she had a rash. She continued to sob until she heard the hum again.

She wobbled up, the threads guiding her through the room. Clicking took the humming's place. It rattled through the halls, settling in her bones. She wasn't sure where it had come from or where it was going. Time trickled down the hourglass that was her dress, slowed. The red sands of her threads stilled themselves, making her listen.

The clicking jerked, cracking its neck, before dying. Whispers entered her mind, floating through. Some told her how to escape the winding halls and cracked door frames. Others begged her to stay, in an orchestra of caterwauls. They wanted her to keep their rotting wood company, care for their peeling skin and broken joints. Some made promises, promises to stop the insufferable bugs that laid themselves under her skin. They promised to give her a crescent moon, a charm to rid her of sickness and bad luck. Chantilly didn't want their promises. She didn't want to save them from their grief. She wanted to leave! She wanted to listen to those whispers about getting out. But they were drowning. Why couldn't they just let her leave? This desperation melted itself into her bones.

Another voice burst through, not only within her, but in the marrow of the room. It rattled its skin, thorns ripping through to give the voice a home. A broken puppet fell from the ceiling, strung up by threads that jerked its limbs, awkward and horrible. Cracking like shattering bones followed with every movement. She stepped back from the creature as it approached her, dangling, relentless.

"Why…? Why are you using your horrid voice here? Did we ask you to speak? No no no, shut up. Leave? Leave, no you can't." Layers of crying hyenas rocketed through her like wires slicing through her organs. The joints cracked and splintered with every word. More voices joined it, echoing every word spoken. Some mocked her voice, some the voice of the puppeteered creature. The booming threatened to blow out her ears.

Chantilly watched the torn skin and ragged clothes break forward, five voices speaking out of it, all in cacophony. She was to go insane, that was all there was to it. The voices screamed at her to stop all this nonsense, to grow up, she couldn't leave, was she stupid!? She was trapped here, she shouldn't have come in if she wanted to leave. Chantilly scoured for an escape, the cracks growing closer.

The room was closing in on her, shortening the distance between her and the skin walls. The threads returned to haunt her as they stretched out of her skin, plunging into the flesh of the wallpaper to play puppet with her. It had her. Her limbs moved to odd angles, bones snapping to tear at muscle and tissue. She was pushed into the mass of the dolls. The creature hung in front of her. She could smell the cool rot dripping off of it. Mold and insects crawled out of its deteriorating skin, centipedes writhing from the eye sockets, back into the mouth and ears. Was she to be like this too?

Chantilly didn't want to be a creature that breathed with five voices, all wanting different things. Softer voices begged for her to go, while the stronger ones condemned her for daring to want to leave.

Chantilly tried to run, only to be pulled back by her string controllers. This wasn't her body anymore, all she had was her mind. Even that was being stolen from her. Voices pierced through her mind, aided by the rotting monster. She screamed and sobbed, fighting the threads, squeezing her eyes shut until everything was silent again.

Opening them, she found she wasn't in the hall anymore, but a huge room with a pond. It was set up to look like the outside; walls stretched to the heavens, painted universes before her eyes. The pond roared like the sea, soft and comforting. It was dangerous, yet she was drawn to the ominous solace of the place. She let it wash over her like a cool rain. Unlike the others, it only spoke with one voice, only one sentence, "You can leave where the stars meet the sea."

Her heart sank. Chantilly was confused. The voice left her with nothing more, to the mercy of the threads and shrieking voices that shattered her mind. She didn't understand, but she had to leave. She'd do anything to go, yet the eerie experience left her craving answers.

She remained hung by her strings, not sure if she could unravel from them. They held onto her bones and joints like a fiery poison setting light to her veins, killing her from the inside out. She struggled against them, she didn't want to be a puppet, a toy to be manipulated and ogled at. Chantilly inhaled, building what strength she could to break free from this poison.

She cried, hot tears running down her cheeks, her limbs moving in their own horrible crack, muffled by her skin and muscle. They moved at strange angles, scrambling of their own accord until all her strings were tangled, and she was a broken toy. Like rope held to a candle, her strings snapped.

She plunged into the pond below.

She could breathe, but no air entered her lungs no matter how much she drank at it. She kept plunging further into the water, doll bodies decorated with golden crowns and jewelry followed after her. She was dragged down by her dress, which was still ticking away the seconds. She could leave when the stars met with the sea, was such a thing possible? She almost didn't think so.

Black water swam around her, to carry her wherever it so pleased. Her eyes flickered to a close when the dolls grabbed onto her, humming their songs in her head. They pulled at her, yanking her wires. Weaving them in and out of her organs, keeping her together by mere threads. Looking out into the black water, she listened to the voices:

"Look. look at them, look at the water. Isn't it pretty?"

"How could you close your eyes? You'll miss it."

"You broke your strings simply to sleep? Why do it at all?"

They asked with burning curiosity, such as her own had been.

Looking out, she saw it: a universe. Star-speckled fish swam through her. Galaxies danced in her hair. They cut off her hearing. The dolls melted away into the black water.

Where the sea meets the stars, it was suffocatingly beautiful.

The beauty didn't last. Soon, it melted away like gold.

The warmth of her escape was dashed. The red threads returned to wrench her back. They snagged her so far down she was sure the pool was endless.

It was dark.

The universe was taken from her too soon.

The waltz continued.

—Annabella Hill

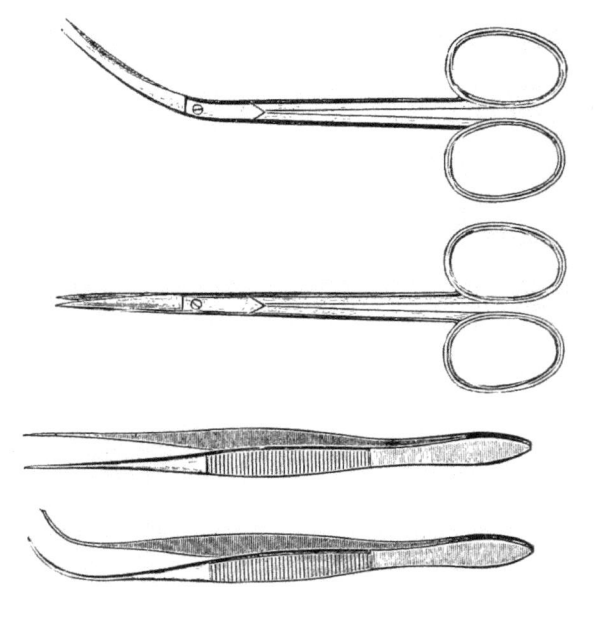

SATYA KUTSKO

STUCK

My eyes flutter open, but I don't see anything. I'm lying down. The bed is soft, but not mine. I blink into pure black. And it is silent. Silence consuming everything around. Right next to my ear, a light switch is pulled, the sound shooting a surge of shock down my spine. Then, silence. The light is a dim cyan. It's held by a metal shade and wire going up to god knows where.

But the light is the perfect dim; not light enough for me to see the whole room, just light enough for me to see what's close. It swings, and makes no noise.

Silence.

A swallowing silence, so that I can't even hear my heartbeat in my ears, or feel it in my breath. I can't move.

Some force I cannot identify is pulling me down. I try to move my arms, my legs, and I try to wiggle my fingers and toes, but still nothing. Hey—I try to say—Hey. I feel the vocal vibration in my throat.

The silence is so large it rings.

Paralyzed but alert, I try to move, again. I shake, scream, but remain motionless, silent, stuck. The ringing grows and grows. The light is swinging in large circles. I cry out, and swallow the feel of it like gravel in my throat. There is only silence. I lay my head down, turning to the left, sensing the wounds of my howling opening in my chords. There's a ringing in my ear.

I move…

The circular light swings overhead. I lift my eyelids. There's someone lying there, 12 inches away from my face. The face and figure are so ambiguous. I may have seen them before, but I can't tell. They're so thin that they are nearly a skeleton. Cloaked in an oversized gown. Their pallid face caving into their mouth. Their lips are dry, chapped, and slightly parted. A cold, scentless breath blows out of the mouth. Their sharp cheekbones threaten to cut the skin. Their hair is covered by a dirty gray wool beanie.

And the eyes.

My god, those eyes. Dead, already glassed over. The irises were a cool gray, their exterior was faintly bloodshot. The pupils were small and surrounded by terror. Strange tears poured down the face, wetting the pillow. The eyes weren't looking at me. They were staring at something behind me. Chills spread through my body.

Hey, it's okay.

Not a sound.

It's gonna be fine, everything will be alright.

I repeat over and over again, the ringing in my ears gets louder and louder.

Something else in the room. A sound. A heart monitor—

Beep…beep…beep…

I scream and scream. Still nothing comes out. The tears still flowing. I cannot move. The heart monitor grows faster until—

Blackout.

Silence returns.

I see nothing but those eyes, illuminated in the darkness. Their irises slowly trickle down to stare directly into mine. They whimper, in a gravelly, broken voice.

I'm sorry...

A flatline fills the room. Lifeless eyes staring into mine. I shake and shake and blink and move, but I'm stuck there, staring endlessly into their eyes.

Stuck.

—Satya Kutsko

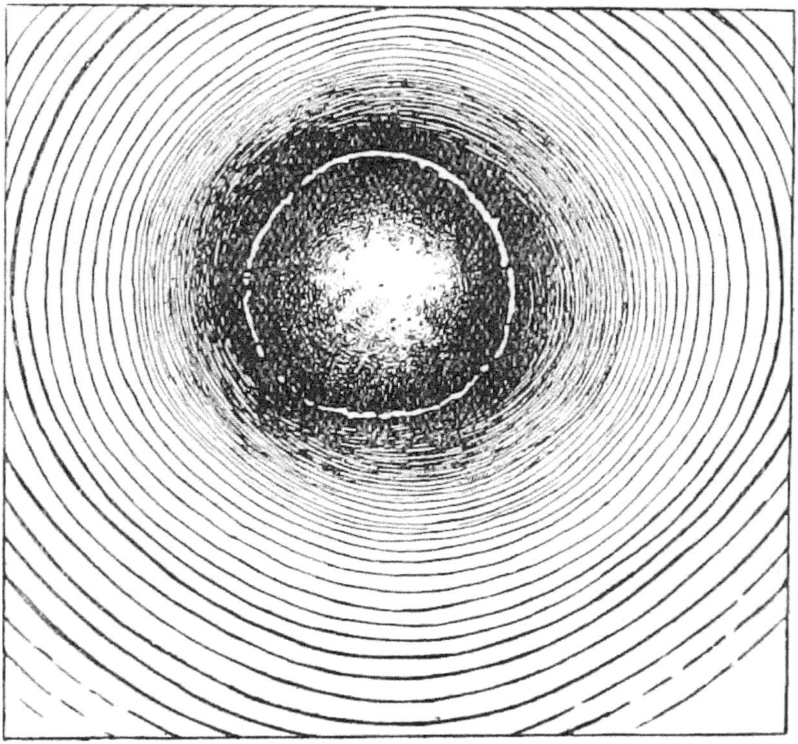

GABRIEL BOSTON-FRIEDMAN

4 POEMS

THAT WORD

That Word
You said it 100 times   in your head
 sniffed out every variable of pronunciation
  you could imagine.
It possesses a slight fragrance of old cowboy boot
  with a voice of confidence, self-esteem
but you didn't look it up, you just assume its meaning
  through observations.
You just rehearse it till you assume that it is ingrained
  in your memory for eternity
  praying that when on stage
  it will be there.
Words are always accessible when you are under pressure
Get on stage...

Before you can even speak your pits stink of salt
  sweat drips down your body.
Your fear of sour embarrassment takes the better of you
Your intense dread of the Word you don't know fills you
Focus exclusively on the page...

You recite the manuscript as you rehearsed
Words melt into lava and ooze to sea
The poem unfolds off your tongue in a swift river
    current of magma.
Come to that Word
The one you resisted diligently   in your head

You stumble over it
but you don't catch your fall
plummet headlong to the ground
busting your nose on the hard truth
blurting out a few words that you sense are right
a cacophony of nonsense that shatters the serenity of the poem
words not included in the repertoire you practiced
tongue writhes   surges stumbling
for a pronunciation it recognizes
anticipating the rewarding taste of sweet success
    only to give up
hoping that at least one of those words was sufficient
and the audience will still get the overall gist
but even if it was adequate
it wouldn't be for you
That Word will reverberate endlessly in your mind
    till the end of time, because
    you took one word
pronounced it a different way each time you said it
and you still don't know what it means.

FUTURES

The world flies in front of me in one fleeting second.
In that moment, all the birds who have wings to fly
have been spooked and have all at once darted
into the sky, disturbing the air in their haste.
They come back after going nowhere
sitting in the same exact place.
And nothing is lost,
except this world
which has gone
nowhere.

ENDLESS DESTINATIONS

How you got here
You don't know.
Where you are going,
You don't know.
Where you will end up,
You will find out.

You arrived where you are
On a rocky plateau.
Your path vanished without a proper farewell.
Leaving you in a limitless expanse.
With the wood behind you,
You venture into the rocky unknown.
You climb over new rocks,
Plants clawing at your legs,
Replacing flesh with air.

Last night you slept by a glacier lake.
When you dipped your feet into the icy water
Energy rushed through you
Until you went numb.
You crawled to the safety of your towel
Away from the same fear you face today.

Now you move towards the mysterious horizon,
As it tears away at your eternally replenished curiosity.
The endless plateau drops off, giving way to new emotion.

You are going in the right direction
To a parking lot where you left your car before embarking on this
 unpredictable journey.
You enjoyed it, and will always remember this adventure.
You do want a bed for the night, so the sooner you can get back to
 your car would be great.
After sleeping on a rock plateau, with nothing, but frozen lake and
 a helicopter landing.

You just came from a mountain top ridge,
And a summer snow patch.
You took your anger out on the snow.
You tightened the snow in your fist,
Until your hand went numb in the cold.
Now your creation of hate lies shattered,
That perfect orb you made of it.

Now you reach the end of your endless expanse.
You know that you could scale this final cliff.
No one will let you though.

You look down into a meadow,
Past the trees,
To the parking lot,
And start again.

WHAT HAPPENS WHEN YOU ASK QUESTIONS

        What Happens When You Ask Questions?
            World is Subjective
Q. Is this related to my life?
    A. YES! I have to be open
    to the ideas of others while
    asserting my own.

    THE WORLD IS GOING TO HELL

        Q.   Is this related to my life?
        A.   YES! No one can do
        this alone, we all need
        the support of each other.

Additional Ideas
    See the world with new eyes
        The rain falls to the sea
            In fear you fall
            don't do that
    You understand
Live until you die

        BECAUSE THEN YOU WILL BE DEAD

Wait Before You Go I Have One More Question, I see you are going to block me out
    your mind is set on your personal survival alone
        The man in the moon cries hopeless moonbeams and you just enjoy them

> Just try another process to educate yourself
> Self-deprecation isn't your only option, there are other options too I am sure

The worst thing you can think is that you are doomed along with the earth

It seems like a safe conclusion, but won't actually solve the problem, I assure you

> The bird plummets to its death, not just because of you, but all of us all

> If you want to be a black hole in history, go ahead, but I won't forgive you, ever

> But you won't go waste yourself, just like that, 'cause I will never let you.

TUNE YOUR SURVIVAL SKILLS FOR YOU WILL NEED THEM

INNER RESTRAINTS AND HINDERANCES TO OVERCOME 2

A hand flies to point the way to the beauty in a land of freaks
> The world is in our hand, so don't cringe under its weight and drop it

The universe is at a standstill while time tumbles past in the breeze
It is time to break the barriers and face the truth
> Don't let fear cut you from your comfortable perch

Be ever resilient and solid

> HOW WE ARE SACRIFICING THE WORLD?
>> We can't sustain the silence like a foreboding pause
>>> Call the world to witness the sacrifice
>>>> To this nonexistent god-like figure
>>> Don't be change to a fate you have created
>> Break away and materialize your hopes and dreams

...

THEY ARE YOURS TO KEEP FOREVER, MAKING YOU FREE AND
UNSTOPPABLE

Discarding Hate

Remember the joy and discard the hate
The changed melody will never die
Entrenched in our consciousness for eternity

DON'T WORRY I HAVE A LITTLE MORE TO SAY:

Judgements of good and evil are subjective
    Make your word and outward emotions clear
        To express your feelings accurately
            Remember you will always forget something
                Typically, when you need it most

THE WORLD ISN'T ALWAYS FAIR SO MAKE THE BEST OF IT

—Gabriel Boston-Friedman

SKYE BOWDON

WHAT YOUR COUNTRY CAN DO FOR YOU

I see my grandpa pull up into the yard, driving his oldie. The plush dice hanging from the rear-view mirror swing back and forth. He smiles at me while honking the truck's brassy horn. Pitch-black tires scrawl tracks in the dirt, and loose dust rises into the air. The sun reflects from the vehicle's glazed white surface. Rays of light and my grandfather's wrinkled hands steer life back into the old 1963 Ford truck.

Although Ford trucks are widely used today, the original intention for creating them was to meet the utilitarian needs of Americans residing in rural communities. My grandfather's automobile is a part of the fourth-generation F-series. The F-series was produced from 1948 through 1985, and is one of the most popular Ford series, to date. In 1953, the name for the F-series trucks changed from F-1 to F-100. Today, F-100s are considered high-value classics. I can only imagine the life that my grandpa's pickup truck has lived. I envision the past owners of the vehicle cruising down the streets of Austin or maybe the bumpy dirt roads of Santa Fe, listening to The Beatles' first album *Please Please Me*.

*

John F. Kennedy was the new, young face of the presidency in 1960. Kennedy's progressive stance on civil rights, goals of eradicating poverty and winning the Cold War spoke to Americans yearning for a hopeful future. President Kennedy reached out to citizens, asking them to help him raise the country into a better tomorrow. In his inaugural address the president said, "Ask not what your country can do for you; ask what you can do for your country."

✷

I sat on my grandpa's floral-print couch with him as *The Andy Griffith Show*'s theme song came on. The sounds of whistling and band instruments set an exuberant tone, while the screen displayed Andy walking his son Opie down to the fishing hole. I knew the song by heart, and whistled along. The show felt like a time capsule, and I could see it in my grandpa's eyes that watching these reruns was like holding all the time that had passed in his bare hands. An unusual sense of nostalgia washed over me as I observed those years I hadn't been alive to witness in-person. *The Andy Griffith Show* was a wholesome family series that ran on CBS from October 3, 1960 to April 1, 1968. Originally, the show came out in black and white, and it continued that way for 159 episodes, before transitioning to color for another 90 episodes. The show follows Sheriff Andy Taylor in the small North Carolina town of Mayberry.

✷

November 22, 1963. President John F. Kennedy was riding in a motorcade, campaigning in Dallas, Texas. At 12:30 p.m., shots were fired while the Lincoln Continental limousine that bore the president turned past the school book depository in Dealey Plaza.

The assassin shot two round-nose, copper-jacketed 6.5 millimeter rounds. The weapon was an imported war surplus rifle, an Italian Carcano Fucile di Fanteria Mod. 91/38 fitted with a scope. The rifle was purchased eight months prior to the murder of President Kennedy from Klein's Sporting Goods for only $19.95.

✷

The Andy Griffiths Show illustrated moral qualities of empathy, a strong work ethic, and honesty, to an audience of both children and adults. The show did this by simply depicting the average small-town American life. Though I believe that the media holds a strong influence over people, it's up for debate whether or not *The Andy Griffith Show* actually had a positive effect on the character of its viewers. That said, it is also worth considering, as programs like this one have grown scarce, whether the morals that come with them are fading out of society as well?

✷

The president was struck in the neck and head. He was then rushed to Parkland Memorial Hospital. President John F. Kennedy was pronounced dead at 1:00 p.m. It was found that the beloved president was killed by former marine and American communist, Lee Harvey Oswald. On November 25, 1963, the president was carried, in a flag-covered casket, to his burial site at Arlington National Cemetery. On his grave site, today, burns an eternal flame.

—*Skye Bowdon*

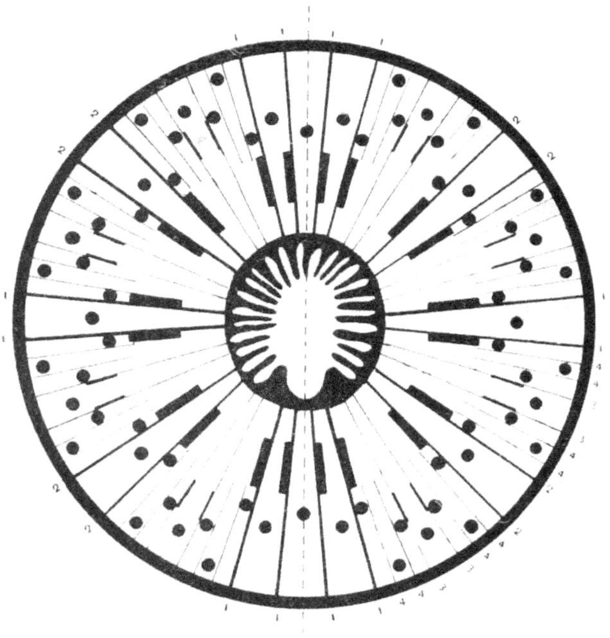

MALIA SEVA

UNTITLED

Two men watch the mountain, parked on the side of the airport freeway. They rest their beers and their bones on the mouth of their tiny van. And we watch them on the strip of park between two freeways. All itch and sunburn. And two men watch us on idling motorcycles. Beat up from the heat and the exhaust. And two mothers watch them from their screened, jailed porch. And who is left to watch them, but the dog.

—Malia Seva

END

STALKING HORSE PRESS is an independent small press, based in Santa Fe, New Mexico. The press was founded by author James Reich, with the intention of supporting innovative and developing voices in contemporary American literature.

www.stalkinghorsepress.com

www.jamesreichbooks.com

NEW MEXICO SCHOOL FOR THE ARTS (NMSA), based in Santa Fe, is the only four-year, statewide, public high school serving artist-scholars across New Mexico with a rigorous, award-winning pre-professional arts and academics program.

NMSA provides students in 9th through 12th grades with intensive, pre-professional instruction in five major arts disciplines, Creative Writing & Literature, Dance, Music (Vocal, Jazz or Instrumental), Theatre, and Visual Arts. Arts disciplines are taught daily by master teachers and professional artists in a 3-hour daily arts block that takes place after the academic day.

NMSA is open to all students in New Mexico who qualify through a blind, competitive audition and portfolio admissions process held every February. Students can audition in up to two of the five major departments. A panel of professional artists participate as part the selection team.

Named as one of the top 10 high schools in the state for 2018 by U.S. News and World Report, NMSA has been a recipient of one of the highest national honors in education, the national Blue Ribbon Award; has received an 'A' grade by the New Mexico Public Education Dept. every year since 2012; and has outperformed for the past five years on state standards assessments in reading, math and science.

NMSA provides a Sunday-Thursday Residential Program to students who live too far away for the daily commute.

NMSA's ethnically and socioeconomically diverse student body hails from 39 communities/Pueblos and a majority of the school's 250 students are minorities.

THANK YOU FOR YOUR SUPPORT.

CPSIA information can be obtained
at www.ICGtesting.com
Printed in the USA
BVHW031211180520
579846BV00005BA/790

9 781734 012613